Elvis in the Lake

...and Other Stories

Eunice Beavers

PublishAmerica
Baltimore

© 2006 by Eunice Beavers.
All rights reserved. No part of this book may be reproduced, stored in a retrieval system or transmitted in any form or by any means without the prior written permission of the publishers, except by a reviewer who may quote brief passages in a review to be printed in a newspaper, magazine or journal.

First printing

At the specific preference of the author, PublishAmerica allowed this work to remain exactly as the author intended, verbatim, without editorial input.

ISBN: 1-4241-1851-4
PUBLISHED BY PUBLISHAMERICA, LLLP
www.publishamerica.com
Baltimore

Printed in the United States of America

Dedication

This book is dedicated
to the memory of
my parents Carl and Merle
and my brother Ralph
and
to
my husband Wayne
and
our daughter Jennifer
for
all their love and encouragement.

CONTENTS

ELVIS IN THE LAKE	7
CATERPILLAR MOUNTAIN	25
A LOTTA WOMAN	43
WILD ONIONS	64
MIRROR, MIRROR	77
RACE TO THE RIVER	93
A MAN ON THE PLACE	114
SOMETHING GOOD	138

ELVIS IN THE LAKE

"Lay, will you rake out the plate scraps for Buddy?" my mother's soft voice requested.

That late June day in the nineteen seventies had not been as hot as some, and there had been no gardening chores, due to a lull between the appearance of early vegetables and late ones. So I was glad to help Mama however I could, and the simple task held considerable contentment.

I made a grand supper for the old hound out of the meat bits, butterbeans, and potatoes that had been left on our four plates, mixed with a handful of his bagged dog food, and topped off with fresh water and a generous amount of hugging. It was a treat for me as well as for the aging dog. "Good boy, you good boy," I murmured into one floppy ear, and received a happy licking in thanks.

Supper had been late that evening, but as my father and I left the kitchen and my mother for the coolness of the front porch, some daylight lingered. Darkness was encroaching, though, and I looked forward to the usual nightly routine.

"Delicious supper, Maggie," my daddy whispered over Mama's shoulder, and planted a quick kiss in her hair as she smiled. Thinking I didn't see, he whacked her tenderly on the rear.

Daddy's pleasant, lined face was illuminated briefly by an after-supper roll-your-own he was lighting. The familiar squeaks of his metal chair told the usual tale. Enough noise and a comfortable position, and he would be there until Mama started closing the living room window that opened onto the porch. She did whatever she did that kept her in the house when Daddy had company. Well, it wasn't really company. It was Uncle A.B., who had already found the wicker rocker and picked Susie off to hold in his lap while he settled into the drowsy gray cat's warmed spot.

Soon Daddy was sliding deeper and deeper into the easy cadences of a conversation with his Uncle A.B., who delighted in discussing politics. Since his wife, my daddy's Aunt Willie, died, Uncle A.B. had come up from his Tennessee home place over by Union City to live with us. Mama put up with him and pretty much stayed out of his way as he did hers, but Daddy thought the world of Uncle A.B. They both seemed to like nothing better than sitting outside, late into a summer evening, engaged in a confab about some political who-knows-what. The talk wafted gently over me, along with the sweet burley smell of Daddy's smoke.

I floated on the rhythm of their voices, riding on the words and the coughs and even the clearing of throats. For the time being, this adventure suited me well.

"...this here all-fired guvmint railroadin' all over everybody..."

"At least we got one from down here someplace close...well, not Kentucky, of course, but the South," my father's voice said gently.

"Hmph," came the gruff reply from A.B.

Daddy amiably continued on, "...though I don't recollect ever knowing anybody from just exactly that part of Georgia...Plains, is it?"

"...like as not he'll be just as bad as the others...can't trust none of them Democrats ner Republicans neither..." asserted Uncle A.B. with a wicked snort.

They were happily entertained and entertaining. I knew Daddy was involved for the duration, so I busied myself with watching the stars come out a few at a time and with considering the beauty of the display. Not much was necessary to occupy my time. I was used to long, quiet evenings at home. My world was safe and comfortable, and I even liked hearing the sound of Uncle A.B.'s thin, croaky voice and seeing Daddy's cigarette fire moving back and forth. Both bare feet on one dewy rail, I balanced myself on the banister and rested my head against a wooden post. This was all I needed to be happy.

But my cousin Warren had a way of changing my life.

"Hey, Layton, race you to the lake!" I heard a voice passing through the dusk.

From my lounging perch, I saw Warren running barefoot down the dirt path that ran between my folks' place and his. Contented as I was to soak up the promised porch conversation, the sight of him hurrying boldly through a midsummer evening toward some as yet unnamed adventure was enough to pull me along, so I slid to the ground and tried to catch up.

We slipped gleefully through a darkening landscape of clipped hay fields and dusty gardens and raced headlong toward the water. Warren's five-months-younger legs still outstretching mine, we tumbled half-laughing, half-gulping for air in a good-spirited chase for the body of water that local people called a lake.

It was not much more than a pond, really, but there was a curve to it, and a compelling size. What truly made it a lake for me, though, was the pier that Jimmy Dawson's grandfather had built at the near side of the curve. Willows that hugged the water's edge, combined with the massive old dock and an intriguing bend just past the dark oak structure, gave the ordinary pond a forever look. Since the other side of the pond could not be seen, there was no telling what might be right around the bend. In fact, there might not have been any limit to the water at all. Maybe it flowed endlessly, until it emptied somewhere like the Gulf of Mexico.

The race halted abruptly, when Warren fell and then righted himself quickly, but with a curse at the bony undergrowth that had tripped him. It was no great problem for me to stop, as I had been straining to keep up anyway.

We were at that perfect spot, where the crowding trees and the pier were silhouetted, black on gold, against the moonlit, ageless body of water. From this angle the bend was in its right place, too, blocking all view of any distant shoreline. What was visible of the water beyond the now outlined pier reflected in its shimmers and ripples only half of a platinum moon. The remainder of the pale disk flickered tantalizingly from between leafy tree branches and infinity.

"Warren?" I huffed, still trying to catch my breath. There was no answer, just some mild swearing, but not at me.

"Warren?" I tried again. "Do you ever think about the lake? I mean, do you ever imagine that it doesn't stop here, that it goes on forever, or at least all the way to New Orleans?"

We were cousins and friends, but without cruelty Warren always managed to make me feel awkward when I delivered myself of some original pronouncement or other, mainly because I had no smoothness or practice at conversation. With my dog Buddy, now, it was different. I was considered extremely wise by that very intelligent being.

This time, though, I could tell I had Warren's attention. As my eyes adjusted to the moonlit dusk, I saw him sitting with feet together and his forearms resting on parted knees. He reached down to massage his sore foot, but trained a skeptical look on me. With my slowly improving night vision, I saw that he tried to scowl but at the same time tried not to grin. The effect was that he did indeed think I was an idiot, but I continued anyway.

"I mean, don't you ever just think of that? It would be so neat to think you could just start out here, in the middle of nowhere, and go on and on and on, and end up..."

I stopped. Even I knew that if anything was going on and on and on, I must be it, so I waited for Warren's ridicule, glad at least that he couldn't see my face fully in the gathering dark.

His answer started to confirm my self-abuse.

"What in the world are you talking about? Sometimes, Layton Stiles, you say the craziest stuff."

Then Warren surprised me.

Still rubbing his offended right foot, Warren seemed to consider my remarks, almost as if I actually had sense and could be taken seriously.

"You know, Lay," he began deliberately, "I never thought of it, but it's like behind a mirror or up behind the moon. No one can say exactly what's on the other side of those things, or even at the end of this water." He paused, then soberly drew his conclusion, "so, whatever you imagine, even if somebody thinks you're wrong, they can't really prove it, and it's all yours to say and believe."

I decided that he must be a genius, being that he agreed with me.

Suddenly the genius rose to his feet, dusted off his rear, and became a scruffy twelve-year-old again.

"But I never figured you to be smart enough to figure that out," he threw back as he clambered down the short bank to the slippery dock.

"Warren, you good-for-nothing!" It was the strongest epithet that my unpracticed tongue could produce. "You wait! I'll show you who's not too smart!" I scrambled to where Warren already perched on the edge of the dark, wet wood pier and dangled his feet in the water.

My plan, maybe, was to shove him in, horseplay and yell and cuss and laugh out loud, like brothers, only better. But I lost my intent when I saw that Warren was staring quietly across the lake.

I pretended not to notice that Warren had rolled up his slightly belled pant legs, and just to show I wasn't copying him, I didn't roll up my overalls legs until I had wet them by plunging my feet straight into the cold water, making sure not to flinch. Then I casually and with great difficulty folded the dark, sodden denim, thinking how stupid my decision had been.

We sat for a time without talking, and I carefully made circles in the water with my big toe. Warren finally broke the silence.

"That's so dumb."

The comment was not unusual. What especially dumb thing had I done now?

But I was not the target.

"Cripes, why did they build a dock out here on this old pond? It's dumb if you're not going to have a pretty big boat or a bunch of them, and even then, they'd just be stuck here on this piddling little pond. And, yeah, yeah, I know you're going to start that crap again about how it really doesn't end here, how it goes on to the ocean, or New Orleans anyway," he mocked. Warren's face was only half visible in the pale moonlight, but I could see a twist to his features.

I did not know how to answer. Didn't he remember his own pronouncement, about how a person could dream about the back side of the moon or the never-ending water?

Warren seemed to hear my confusion. He half-turned toward me with the light framing his head, his profile no longer there for me to read. He studied me a while, then resumed his unseeing search across the gently moving liquid surface.

Eventually I summoned a speck of bravery.

"Yeah, I guess it is piddling," I lied. It was anything but that to me, but I decided to choose my battle. "And I know there aren't any boats..." I began.

Warren's silhouette had not changed. I plowed on.

"...But maybe it has something else special of its very own, besides the stuff about New Orleans, even." I waited, hoping I wasn't talking just to the trees and the water.

"Like what?" he managed, his vision still fixed on some point neither above nor below the gleaming surface.

"Well...," I searched for an answer, and then saw it in the moonlit water. Quickly scooping a handful of small stones and their attendant trash, I hurled the combination a few yards out into the gentle pond, which reacted predictably. Pointing with my emptied hand at the disturbance, I continued, "...just look at how those ripples move. It's like they're waving, maybe sort of like dancing..."

I hesitated, but Warren made no response.

"Warren, look! See how they're wiggling like that, back and forth," I demanded. This time I was successful; Warren's head moved ever so slightly and I could tell he was looking in the direction of the shimmering, ever-changing circles in the pond. This was it. I said, "It's like Elvis, shimmying and quivering like he does when he sings, like on TV."

That got his notice. With his head framed by the backlight, Warren turned his invisible gaze on me again. I knew my face was exposed, and maybe my stupidity as well, but I just stared right back as though I could see him.

The words came slowly, thoughtfully. "Yeah...yeah..." he spoke first to me and then, turning to the water with something akin to respect, "...maybe it is. Maybe so. Yeah, like Elvis in the lake." He sounded surprised, even impressed, by the entertaining idea.

"I never woulda seen it, but yeah, look at it!" Warren's voice sounded happy, and then he made a goofy act of playing a guitar, tossing his head back and forth. He splashed his feet in the water and wailed, "Blue-oo-ah-hoo, blue suede shoes! Blue-oo-ah-hoo, blue suede shoes!"

We guffawed at his performance, Warren laughing as uncontrollably as I. He repeated the act, adding more and more wild air guitar licks and shaking his bony pelvis on the wet dock. When we calmed down, after several tries, we sat and watched the still annoyed pond surface shudder and mutter and simmer until it had almost settled back down.

It was getting late and Mama would be closing the living room window, and I needed to go home, but I was satisfied. Warren had seen what I had seen. The view was a secret between us, a shared, cousinly secret that we had, like some people have a club or a treehouse. I didn't have those things, but I had a special lake that moved like the King himself and then went on to the ocean itself. And Warren had seen it, too.

Warren sprang to his feet without announcement. I waited a respectable time, then got up myself. We headed single file back toward our homes, away from the water, away from Elvis. I ambled along with a light heart, stepping to the rhythm of croaking frogs and other splashing pond life. Life was good and I had a lifelong friend.

The next few weeks I saw scarcely any people my age. The truck crop that my family raised kept us especially busy in late July, as tomatoes and corn had to be kept up with daily. One incompletely filled-out ear of corn would kill the potential sale of a few dozen ears, and tomatoes that developed soft spots and a rotten smell could taint all the others in a bin.

We would "set up" at the local farmers' market at an old sock factory warehouse lot in the washed air of early morning and have a great day, in my opinion. I enjoyed the sorting and the selling and developed a certain pride in the way our wares were presented. The other sellers were accompanied by their children of assorted ages, most of them much younger than my thirteen years, but I actually worked while the others just ran around. It was a good feeling to be considered responsible. I was more than satisfied with my days spent in dusty jeans and faded shirts until Warren changed my world again one day.

Parched from a morning's work in the heat, I swung out of the rough-covered front seat of Daddy's battered Ford pickup truck to run into Mister Dunning's store to get each of us a cold Coca-Cola. Happy anyway with my fulfilling summer role with the vegetables, I was even happier with the chance to get the drinks, just as if it was something I did all the time. Mister Dunning's slow screen door had barely slapped-to behind me, and I had already held up my two fingers and swapped the few coins for "a coupla Cokes" when I heard the giggles.

"Hiiii, Layyyton," came a sweetly singsongy female voice. I was still blinking from the early afternoon sun as I made out the shapes in one of two red vinyl booths that this small grocery afforded its occasional lunching customers.

"Hi," I said casually, as if I knew to whom I was speaking. The musical voice did seem to be attaching itself to a wondrous creature with side-parted, glistening, long hair.

Beverly Madison smiled from a beautiful face framed in silk and, to the grins and stifled laughter of her boothmates (Warren's sister Debbie and Sandra somebody), patted the rounded seat-half beside her and invited, "Why doncha come over here and drink your Coke with us?"

I stood amazed, with Daddy's and my frosty bottles starting to make my dusty palms muddy. Gripping the ridged glass harder, I hoped I wouldn't drip brown spots on the clean black and white tile. In a flash of awareness, I was sharply conscious of my country-boy appearance and my streaked, thin face with big ears and dry-straw hair. Sandra-somebody was looking me up and down with undisguised disgust. My cousin Debbie would have died rather than admit to kinship, so I made up my mind to ignore her, too. I detected a slight movement under the table as Beverly's foot nudged her friends into playing by the rules. Beverly patted the seat again.

"No, I mean, I guess, I can't," I struggled. "I mean, my daddy's waiting." Great! Couldn't I at least have said "family" instead of the baby-sounding "daddy" or even better, "truck," as if I had arrived alone?

The bottles seriously began to sweat, and syrupy stains started from my wrists down my upward-bent forearms. Sandra barely suppressed a snort of derision, and got a swift kick from Beverly for her opinion. I decided it was time to escape.

"Well, 'bye, now. Thanks anyway. Some other time?" I tossed off the words in what I hoped was an everyday line, used on many, many occasions when beautiful girls wanted my valuable time.

My escape had almost been accomplished, and I had even turned my eyes from the pretty, heart-shaped face, when I heard the words that had to have come from Warren.

"But, Elllllvis! We want you to stay!" The words were accompanied by false swooning as Debbie and Sandra played the backup chorus to Beverly's pouting imitation of a pleading fan. "Please, please, please," they all joined in, "please sing for us!" They took turns pretending to pass out in fits of excitement.

Beverly made a deliberate stab. "Now, come on, Layton, you know you can do it, like you told Warren down by the lake all about how the water shimmies and shakes like Elvis?" She paused only long enough to draw her breath and head in for the kill. "You know, that biiiig old lake that just goes on and on and on and on…" Her chorus did a Motown duo, swaying to the "on's" with their hands making great waves in the air.

Standing glued in place, I saw Mister Dunning's eyes go from my fast-warming bottles down to the puddles that were forming on his floor. I managed to do something like a shrug, probably just another silly move for them to laugh at, and fled to the truck. Daddy took forever to start the motor and even longer to shift into gear. Although the air was breathlessly hot, the burning I felt had nothing to do with the July sun.

There was always work to do on our place, and I had always done my share willingly and even gladly, for I had taken pleasure in my existence up until then. In the days after the store encounter and since my total betrayal by Warren, and my sickened realization that I was a complete and sissy fool in my own and everyone else's eyes, I threw myself into the chores. Daddy would have had reason to be happy with my productiveness, except that I knew he could see something was wrong. To his blessed credit, he never brought up the subject. I appreciated his silence and could never have told him why.

As summer wound down, I could find fewer ways to busy myself away from the company of others my age—as if they wanted to see me—so I concentrated on preparing mentally for eighth grade.

I had thought I would gear up for the year the way I had for school in the past, with a rising degree of anticipation and joy at being able to see friends, both students and teachers, and rejoining a community I felt a happy part of. Classes and assemblies and games made a seamless fabric that I had longed to wrap myself in. Sunny late summer and autumn afternoons were to be spent running to catch a football, falling into leaves, wrestling with other happy, laughing kids, and then running home and over at the mouth to tell Mama what all had happened as she served up a sandwich and a smile.

It wouldn't be like that any more.

When school began, I wasn't there. Oh, I attended and answered the roll call, and did my work and even did it fairly well. No reason to have attention called to me for being either very bad or very good. But I wasn't really there; I stood on the outside and hardly looked in.

No luck, though. Even in the first few days, I was noticed, and I had a new name: "Elvis." I had to admit to feeling a kinship with the poor, lonely boy from not so far down the Southern road. Someplace I read that he was a loner at times, that he didn't fit in, that the "popular" ones didn't include him except for the way he could sing at their assemblies. Well, I couldn't even do that, so I wouldn't be their performing bear at least.

Besides, Warren, who had become one of the favored group, led his new-found friends in providing the sound track to my misery. I often heard "Blue-hoo-ah-hoo, blue suede shoes!" as I trudged down the hallways past their cliques.

I considered doing something to get back at Warren, especially since his very own actions were the ones he presented as having been mine instead, the silly concert by the lake, the physical imitation of the water's movement. But I knew that my efforts would fall flat. Who would believe me? I would just heap more fuel on the fire, if I awkwardly tried to cast their favorite as a villain or buffoon.

So I endured the long, uncomfortable days in silence, in the old brick school with no air conditioning. And I earnestly wished I lived somewhere else besides Kentucky, somewhere that school didn't start so early in the summer, for one thing.

On the seventeenth of this awful month, another hot, hazy August morning dawned about the same as the other pale mornings of my recent days. I had no reason to expect it to be different from any others except that someone would figure out another way to make fun and I would become even more clever at seeming not to care.

I would not be disappointed.

Warren was in fine form this day.

At fifteen before eight, I climbed the ancient concrete steps to the door primly labeled "Junior High." He moved to meet me at the doorway, actually IN the doorway, as I tried to pass nonchalantly between sprawled step-loungers and jersey-clad athletes with the best-looking girls. With a clear air of "Now watch me do this," he half-beckoned to his court to watch, and then unloaded his planned attack.

I saw no one I recognized, certainly not the nice little kid that I had sat beside on a pond pier, or even the laughing cousin whose greatest joy had been to outrun me to win champion of the world or of a spring pasture at least. This somewhat larger, taller version of someone I had once known had an evilly delicious treat for me. He seemed to savor his surprise, strutting a bit before springing it.

"Elvis? Elvis? Hey, where you goin'?" He grabbed my thin jacket, too warm for the weather but another layer of skin for me. "Hey, I'm talkin' to you, CUZ." The old times were indeed forever gone. "Hey, show the girls how you shimmy and shake like the old water-lake!" He made it rhyme.

Faces were turned toward me. I tried to let him have the sleeve of the jacket and to shrink away, far away, inside.

I wanted to pass through, and I didn't want to fight him, but it was getting much harder to remember the old friend I used to have. It didn't even matter to me why he was doing this, and I guess I understood anyway. There had a been a time, a very short time ago, that Warren had been happy on the outside with me, but I guess that was then…

"Blue-hoo-ah-hoo, blue suede shoes! Blue-hoo-ah-hoo,…" he scooped with his left hand to get his crowd to produce the full orchestral effect.

A few nervous giggles escaped, but the concert did not begin.

"Blue-hoo…" Warren hesitated. Looking around with the easy smile that usually ensured his being the center of attention, he seemed to believe that the hesitation was only to allow him the starring turn. His look said, it's all right; you can join me now.

I thought I might pull away, but Warren had tightened his grip on my jacket. Where were his fellow tormentors? Why would they miss practicing on such an easy target?

In the corner of my eye, I caught a heart-shaped blur. Framed in a silky halo, the head was bowed, and then I heard the sound of a girl crying, first one and then others joining in, with a rising murmur of soft talk in the crowd. For one disbelieving moment, I thought the tears were for me, and the ultimate humiliation of having to be defended by a girl, however beautiful, would have been harder to take than the rough treatment that Warren had been dishing out.

As the talk spread and Warren's hand went slack, the realization hit us both about the same time, I think. Beverly and the other girls were weeping, all right, but not for me. The August 16 announcement from Memphis was already three-quarters of a day old, but to me and others whose hours after school were spent in a still more removed world, it was news on this Wednesday morning after.

Even Warren, who had always been the wise and informed one, was blindsided. And he had chosen today of all days to put on his most pointed satire of Elvis Presley, the morning after the king's death. Beverly gulped out the awful truth and told Warren he should be ashamed.

Where we lived, I guess, deepened the effect Elvis's death had on us. He was from Tennessee, not so far from us in southern Kentucky, we would later say to each other, but words were not possible that morning. We could not begin to name, much less understand, the thought of mortality. It was among us, though, and it confused and quieted the young crowd. We stood in silence until the first bell rang.

The crowd thinned, I moved on, and the day limped along with distracted students sitting through classes, until with the afternoon the sounds of youthful play were beginning to work away the grey shroud.

Beverly waited outside my last class. I shifted my book bag to my other side to keep from brushing her as I passed her at the doorway, pretending her presence didn't matter. I was truly not as affected by her as I had thought I would be, probably from my recent practice at not caring. She reached out to touch my upper arm, which I instantly wished had not been so thin. I walked at a regular pace down the short hallway toward the bus lot, with Beverly matching my steps, turned toward me all the way. She wanted to say something, she said, just something about how mean they had all been, and her especially, and how when the news, you know, the news had come, that it was just too sad…

My bus driver was getting ready to jerk the door closed. As I grabbed the handrail, pulling myself onto the bus, I looked down and nodded at Beverly in cool acknowledgment.

From above, just before I landed in the first empty seat, I saw the shiny hair swing downward again. Ah, well, maybe I wouldn't be too hard on her. Although a few tears, some for me even, might be appealing and might even cleanse her soul a bit, I wouldn't want anyone so glorious to suffer for very long. Maybe I would grow my hair a little longer, though. And I wondered how much trouble it would be to learn to curl just one side of my lip. Maybe Warren and I could practice together.

August, 2002

Dottie brought me the paper, smiling as she presented it. "Read the front page," she said, "before the sports or the financial section."

The small feature article from Memphis was in the lower half of the paper, commanding no large audience. "Twenty-five years ago today Elvis Presley was found dead at his Graceland mansion..."

At thirty-eight I became a thirteen-year-old kid again for a few minutes. Dottie's eyes were wise and understanding. She had heard about what Warren had named the "Elvis in the Lake" story many times before.

I picked up the phone and speed-dialed Warren's number. Our regular weekly lunch today will celebrate the memory of an eternal lake with shimmering, moonlit, blue-suede-shoes-shakin' water, and a friendship that has spanned the years.

CATERPILLAR MOUNTAIN

Howard was a man who never cursed God. But now he had done it. With vigor and before 7:00 A.M., and on this beautiful, wide open, heavenly morning. The words had spilled out without warning, threatening the eternal soul of something or other.

Mary's voice, non-accusing, lightly inquiring, floated up to him from where she sat on her white gardening stool. She had only a few overgrown, tough-looking green onions in a pile, from trying to clean out the last leftover spring row of them.

"What did you say, dear?" she said, in the clear, projecting voice of the schoolteacher she would always be. Mary knew what Howard's utterance sounded like, but it couldn't have been.

Must have been "Get down" to some pest on a plant, or "Got one" about a good vegetable. Never the G-D words, she knew. Howard wouldn't say them.

Howard slowly straightened himself, rising tall, and looked down at Mary, her bottom overlapping the primitive wood seat. Her soft red hair shone with silver and sweat. Howard cleared his throat and walked away with as much dignity as he could muster. He did not answer Mary.

Things are changing, he thought. Mary can't hear any more, and I let myself say curse words. Right out here in God's garden, too. Howard carefully placed the offending tool back in its proper notch in the garden shed. The fool thing, a long-handled spade, had nearly cut the toe of his shoe off. Miserable excuse for a piece of equipment, with its rusty spoon and its rough, creaking handle. He decided maybe the cursing was justified.

Howard stretched his thin frame as he stood in the darkness of the shed and wiggled the toes on his recovering right foot. The stretching felt good, but his bones still ached. More and more parts of his body hurt regularly now.

Mary was anchoring herself to rise from the stool. She had to plant her feet wide apart, and she thought he couldn't see. He could, of course, but he pretended he didn't, just like all the other times she had trouble getting up from the sofa and out of the car after a long ride.

"Howard?" Her voice rose slightly as she slowly wiped away perspiration with the clean back of a glove. "Howard?"

He came to the door of the shed.

"Are we through? I've got things to do." Not a complaint, just a statement.

"Might as well. I can't seem to do anything right. And we're both too stiff and sore to be out here," he grunted.

There was a silence, both looking out over the tiny garden, only a remnant of what had been a grand annual effort except for the last few years.

When the back screen door had whapped behind her, Howard stood alone and scratched the stubble that was growing on his lean jaws. He wondered where the day-start had gone.

There were few times that the sun rose before Howard. When it did, he was disappointed, feeling himself cheated of part of his day. He had succeeded earlier this morning, however. Striding boldly with long, bony legs, he had walked out toward the waking sun as it yawned and sputtered sleepily in surprise at having been bested.

The purple martins had still barely cooed when Howard began his customary June-morning garden check. Suspended above the ragged fence row, their many-holed birdhouse teetered gently to the left of the present garden and between a now untended area and the pasture. Their green and white apartment house soon had begun to twitter uneasily, as some alert dwellers on the western side sensed the approach of the monster-man.

Howard had no argument with them, he wanted to say, go back to sleep. While he inched his way through the neat but sparse vegetable rows, the noise lulled somewhat, but there were still a few sounds of chicken-muttering in the precariously leaning tower.

Not a man concerned with the musings of almanac writers, Howard did not recall knowing before the past weekend what a summer solstice was. But Sunday morning's breakfast with Mary had yielded one fact that caught his attention: Today was to be summer's—and the year's—longest day.

She was like that, Mary, always informing on some subject or other, treating him like one of her former students, Howard thought. Many times it was hard listening or pretending to, but once in a while—particularly this time—he did not have to feign the interest he put on his face. Especially when she said *after tomorrow the days'll get shorter a little bit every day pretty soon it'll be winter oh lord I hate to think about winter...*

When he woke before dawn today, the words came repeating themselves in his head: *days'll get shorter...winter winter.* So Howard had determined to rise even earlier than usual, in spite of his bone-cricks, to venture into the damp garden. He had wanted to hold every second, every tiny eyelash-flicker of a world just waking up.

Then here she had come, right out into the dew-wet rows, talking again, oh lord, always talking.

The martins hushed up of a sudden, startled by her noise, then bustled alive and flew out in all directions. Howard's gentleman's agreement with them had not mattered any more. Howard himself did not matter any more.

Now, after thirty minutes or so, Mary had finally gone back into the house and out of his hair.

Since he had it all to himself again, Howard stayed, half hoping to make up for the lost solitude. He lingered too long in the warming garden, but the heat felt good for a while. Then moisture began to form inside the stiff collar of his white cotton shirt. The buttoned long sleeves would have been rolled up by a younger man, or there might have been no shirt at all.

Crouching beside the first squash plant, Howard was again aware of that creakiness and dull joint-ache he seemed to have nearly all the time now. At seventy-two, while the world was filling up with hundred-year-olds for Willard Scott to congratulate, Howard resented the way time and its cohort, nature, ravaged all earthly things, but his flesh in particular.

Howard did not blame God, though. His own ideas on fate were not too thought out, but he figured they would do, as his part didn't matter much anyhow. God must be a businesslike fellow and would know when his human clumps of dirt had worn far enough down, Howard's to be included. He pictured God's big enfolding hand that would come and scoop him up someday.

The tiny flash of anger at nature was therapeutic, though. It helped him put away the queasy feeling that he felt when he rose from crouching. He braced himself, took in a good breath of fresh morning air, and began to check in earnest for the small yellow squashes.

As he worked his way down the row, with the handle of an ancient split oak gathering basket over one arm and the wire bail of a tall plastic bucket in his other hand, he occasionally upended the bucket and sat on it to do his picking. Soon Howard had his carrier almost full of smooth baby squashes and spiny cucumbers. He checked the one tiny green pepper one more time—unlike squash, it did not seem to grow overnight.

Squash, the dusty too-big last of the green onions, cucumbers. That would be all for now. Tomatoes and peppers were coming, but not quite yet. Not a complicated garden, just a simple one, well-spaced and mostly in by late June.

There would be no beans.

Howard did not grow green beans any more; too much trouble when you could get cans so cheap at the TopSaver. So he and Mary said.

"TopSaver has 'em on special for four cans for a dollar," he had observed about every two weeks, especially since the big Dixie Mart had come to town.

"As long as they're that cheap, why stand over a hot canner in August?" had been Mary's standard comment. Both had nodded at the wisdom of their shopping decision.

So they said, but still he missed reaching into a mass of greenery to discover a whole handful of long, deeply colored Kentucky Wonders, their cool firmness a contrast to the plant's scratchy leaves.

The bucket-seat had originally been used for five gallons of pickle slices. Bought empty for fifty cents from the cafeteria at the school where Mary used to teach, it had been kept for years, protected in the dark shed from winter elements and storms. It was Howard's alone, used for sitting on to weed or to gather several vegetables from one plant. Turned bottom up and worked a little into the dirt for a firm mooring, the green plastic container was ideal for relieving his back of much of the necessary bending.

But beans, now, beans would be worth bending for.

But beans were cheaper at the store...

Howard's reflections had cost him more time than he had intended. A martin swooped to within a few feet of his head, informing him that the colony was now more than fully awake and that Howard had moved too close to the fence-row box. Some of the birds made great high circles, looking for breakfast as insects began to chirp in the fields.

The hot, dry feel of day had replaced the cool wetness

of dawn. More of the green plants' freshness was gone, too, Howard observed regretfully as he headed for the house, leaving his garden to the flames of an eternal sun. Nothing could stand this heat for long.

An eastward-facing garden slope and the Barneses' back porch were no places to be on a late June morning in Kentucky. As he washed off at the hydrant, bright sunlight bored into Howard's head, even through the crown of his sweat-circled straw hat.

Ninety degrees of mercury showed by 9:30 on an outdoor thermometer. Hanging askew on one of the clothesline posts, the round white instrument with its large red pointer and black numbers registered the difference between outside heat and inside coolness. Howard sat and sipped strong coffee left from breakfast. Trapped behind the kitchen's gingham-checked veil, he fretted about the passing minutes.

With the fiery ball finally beginning to move overhead to torment the front of the house instead, Howard gathered up his coffee cup and his body aches and moved to the back porch. The baking garden in his view was now no longer his, but the sun's, and his gaze lifted above it. From his perch in a much-painted swing made higher by Mary's accumulation of pillows, he watched the ravaging of old Fuzzy Top.

In its prime, Fuzzy Top could be seen for a few miles each way. Covered with lofty, dark evergreens, the round hill looked higher than it really was.

Howard knew the real Fuzzy Top. He had squirrel-hunted it when he was younger, and it was the tallness of the old trees that had given it an extra authority. Not a mountain like those in eastern Kentucky, it was still just about the supreme vantage point in these western parts of the commonwealth, and the view from where one could stand flatfooted on its crest was a vista of patchworked beauty. Howard smiled at the memory and breathed deeply, as if inhaling that long-ago cedar smell.

From the back of Howard's house it was maybe a mile to the once-beautiful hill. He could see the Caterpillars crawling on it, and occasionally the wind carried a faint droning or chunking sound. Already almost scalped, Fuzzy Top was being devoured. The tiny yellow worms were working away at the remaining green cover, digging into the pale orange flesh. Howard could see the heads of the worms lowering to eat, then backing up to disgorge their mouthfuls. It was too far away to see, but he knew that great mounds of dirt were being spooned up and removed by the yellow machines. Old Fuzzy-Top was no longer worthy of its name.

"You going to Wal-Mart or not?"

Howard jumped. Mary ought not to sneak up on people like that.

"No. Why?" Howard searched for whatever he was supposed to remember.

Mary was quick to remind him. "Well, it's not that I care especially, but you said you'd meet Herbert and Duke there as usual. And I've got a list I've held onto all weekend because you said you were going today. Besides, it's awfully hot. No need of me going if you're going anyway."

Botheration. He couldn't even go and sit and have coffee in the Wal-Mart deli without her giving him a job to do.

"Of course, if you don't want to, I'll just have you drive me in later. Most likely the list will be longer by then."

Mary did not mean it as a threat, but it worked anyway. He dang well did not want to wait on her while she trailed around all over the store. And the deli started filling up before noon during any day on a work week, to where a man would not have much room to just sit and have coffee with friends. People would eye your table, people holding filled trays in their hands and checking their watches. Mondays were especially bad, so he had better go early.

Howard had a cup of coffee and a refill and then had to go to the lavatory. Although it was air-conditioned, the small room felt stuffy. A weak light over the sink glared like the garden sun. Howard was almost sick at his stomach, but he held it. No way would he be a sick old man in the Wal-Mart restroom. They might even announce it over the intercom, well-meaning and all.

Herbert and Duke were not the same as they used to be. Howard had seen things changing for a while, but had not wanted to say anything. Herbert's wife LouAnn had died the winter before last, about eighteen months ago maybe, and he had taken a while to get back out for coffee. Howard and Duke had held onto the informal meeting time, a trifle scared at times that one or the other would not make it, and the habit would be too easily broken.

But Herbert had come back, and things were normal again. The mild winter just past had not had enough snow to prevent their getting together, and the air was only cold enough to be invigorating.

Then Herbert had started courting. A lady had just moved back to McAtee from Florida, where she and her husband had been living prior to his death. Herbert was not at all the same. Duke and Howard had exchanged more than one look about it lately.

"Hoo-ee," wheezed Duke, "look out, now! He won't be sittin' around up here with us much longer, when she marries 'im and starts telling 'im what to do."

Howard and Duke quietly gloated that their wives sure didn't tell them what to do, but Duke did not know that Howard had his number, too. There were just too many references to the expected grandchild. Howard had seen it happen before.

Although he himself had shown around pictures of Beverly's two girls and Alec's son when they were small, they had lived at enough distance that he was not overly attached to them. But those who had grandchildren nearby and had opportunity to dote on them usually did exactly that. Howard could see it coming in Duke's case. Duke and his wife had even fixed up a room at their own home to be a nursery when the baby would be there, he had said.

It was plain that the Wal-Mart mornings with Duke and Herbert were numbered.

Howard's younger son Wilson was married but had no children, and Mary had lamented the lack of local grandchildren, but Howard did not miss what he had not experienced.

"Think about it, Mary. If Wilson and Betty had kids, they wouldn't be able to see about us when we need 'em, like they do. And since at least one of us"—he had jokingly jabbed an index finger at his listening wife—"is getting older, it's good to know that someone will be around to help us when one or the other of us gets down."

Her unsmiling face had given no response.

Wilson was the one who took him on Wednesday morning to see the work on Fuzzy Top up close. Howard had started telling him how he was going to drive out when Wilson suddenly spoke up and said he'd rather Howard didn't drive, that he was going anyway. Howard smelled pity.

"Well, suit yourself," said Wilson calmly, carefully pulling out a chair to his mother's kitchen table, "but I was just telling Momma that I hadn't been out that way since I was learning to drive and I wished you would kind of point out where folks used to live before things change any more." He had hesitated to let his words settle, and then proceeded deliberately, as if he really didn't care, it was just an idea. "I'll ride with you if you're going, but you could point things out better if I drove."

Howard weighed the subtle, too-unconcerned way that Wilson had put the offer, and decided to shrug off the well-meant condescension. He accepted. He could pretend and make Wilson happy. Anyway, Howard looked forward to the freedom to gawk at will.

"Son, you can be glad I'm not like some people around here," Howard remarked as he fastened the seat belt to satisfy his boy, who would fret out loud all the way if he left it unclasped. There were a lot of them, he told Wilson, crotchety old folks, that is, who complained about the Fuzzy Top project. They didn't see the value of the new development that was being planned at its base, with another whole industrial park to get its water and electricity from reservoirs and power plants on what used to be a plain old hill.

Howard was all for progress. He looked forward to listening to the vigorous young engineers when he and Wilson would reach the construction site.

"They'll probably want to know how I feel about the whole thing," he mused aloud as his son drove quietly, "and I'll tell them things that they need to know." They would find in Howard an informed, adaptable sage who could bridge the span between the hill's primitive past and its gleaming, modern future. The past and the future needed to be pulled together, and somehow Howard felt he was the one who should do it.

His father's breathless, rambling urgency was new to Wilson.

Howard planned his words in his mind, "You all prob'ly don't know this, but over there in the distance, that way, that's Salter County. See, over that patch of those harvested winter wheat fields—the real light yellow—there's a little bitty corner of Lester County…"

Howard had gotten to thinking about the way he would describe the view from Fuzzy Top and had let much of the short drive pass without pointing out to his son the old farms on the way. Anyway, there were tiny new houses and the old homeplaces were cut up, so Howard did not feel too certain of where they were passing. At least Wilson did not ask, either, about the landmarks he had said he was so interested in.

They sat a few minutes in Wilson's neat blue Ford, a

respectful distance from the sign that warned unauthorized personnel to stay away.

The noise was deafening when they opened the car doors. What had from a distance been occasional buzzes and clicks became horrid squawks and screeches that became even louder as father and son neared the construction site on foot.

Howard was enthralled. Never had he been this close to the operations of heavy machinery. Powerful and willful, the machines exercised their authority on the mountain, already gouged into submission by earlier feedings.

Wilson aggravated him by supporting his elbow. Hadn't he squirrel-hunted this hill before Wilson, the baby of the three, had even been born? Howard wasn't likely to stumble. Maybe he should brace his son's elbow instead.

"Hold up there!" The voice came from a gaggle of men who stood near one of the dirt-coated machine creatures.

"You there! You don't need to be in this area! There's too much danger!" a muscular man with a different color work uniform from the others half-shouted as he hurried toward Wilson and Howard.

Wilson's arm was already in the crook of Howard's elbow, pulling him toward the Ford. Howard let the gray-shirted man get closer. He could now see the sewn-on label. Under Mid-Tech Construction he saw that the approaching hard-hatted muscleman was the foreman of the project, one G. L. Matlock.

Well, this was exactly as it should be. Howard would introduce himself to the boss in charge. This one could then sort of call the others over to hear an older gentleman who had lived here all his life and, unlike others his age, was a far-seeing and dynamic individual. Howard could absolve them of guilt that others might have forced on them about changing the mountain. He would explain soothingly that there were surely others like himself who understood the needs of progress.

And if they had run up against the naysayers, why, he would be a go-between and he would bring both sides together and would heal the rift between the old and new. He would be acknowledged...

"Get this old man outta here!"

Wilson's hand was pulling obediently.

"Don't you know this old geezer can get hurt up here around all this heavy equipment? Get him gone right now, you hear?"

Wilson's grip was surprisingly strong. He mumbled some humble acquiescence and took hold of Howard's arm with both hands. In a hushed voice he whispered, "Daddy, come on. We better go."

Howard stared. The sun-darkened face of the loud speaker was close now, near enough for Howard to see the bristles and dirt-lined creases that accented the harsh words.

"You hear me, old man?" Matlock's voice rose as though being used for a deaf person. To Wilson he growled, "Get this old coot outta here!" Snickers came from the group around an idling Caterpillar.

Howard had wanted them to follow their foreman's lead, but this rude individual did not seem to understand what Howard could do for the whole crew.

Wilson's pulling almost threw them both off balance.

Howard struggled to get loose, and Wilson, fearful of hurting his father, lost his hold for an instant.

Howard bypassed Matlock, heading straight for the machine and the four workers who stood arrested in amazement at his sudden approach.

"I been here all my life. I squirrel-hunted up here fifty years ago. Did you know you can see part of three counties…"

Howard did not get to finish. He did not even get to connect the old with the new as he had planned. The foreman appeared at his side and jerked him away from the equipment. The dusty young operators scattered and were watching from points several feet away.

The ensuing scuffle between Wilson and the angry grayshirt, with Howard in the middle, was mostly shoving and yelling, but Howard felt himself turning, nearly falling. Sun was in his eyes again, and the dizziness returned. The spinning, like the light in the Wal-Mart john, made his stomach turn.

As Wilson dragged him away, Howard's own voice surprised him, croaking a backwards yell.

Well, that would make it two curses for the week.

Matlock stopped in his stroll back to the slender young workers. He turned, grinning broadly, and to the accompaniment of a chorus of youthful laughter, replied, "Well, 'Good Day!' to you, too. You better watch your language, old man!"

"Good Day!" was certainly not what Howard had said. He opened his mouth to try to correct the foreman's hearing, but he would have been drowned out by the guffaws.

And Wilson had him firmly this time, the son clearly not in the mood to brook any more cussing, especially of the studied-out kind.

Wilson crossly stuffed him into the car and locked and slammed the hot metal door. The window was up, and Howard searched for a crank to lower it, but the car was all automatic. Wilson fell into the driver's seat and started the motor, determined to leave quickly but without spinning gravel. The hot, stagnant air took Howard's breath away. Wilson, however, delayed lowering the windows or turning on the air conditioning. He definitely did not want the vehicle to stall because of too many demands placed on it at once.

His Ford departed the scene at a dignified speed that increased only when the warning signboards receded into the background.

The conversation in the slowly cooling air was one-sided. Wilson, as gentle a man and a son as could be imagined, was angry, and his anger was divided between the foreman and his father.

"That sweaty, loud-mouthed idiot! I'm sure going to let somebody at the courthouse know that we've got people like him working out here on our county land. Plus, they're getting all kinds of puffed-up publicity about how they're doing us such a favor with their so-called improvement!"

Wilson gave his father no time to reply with his usual pie-in-the-sky nonsense about progress and all. Although his hands were clamped tightly onto the steering wheel and his eyes stared straight ahead, Wilson's words now zeroed in on the seat's other occupant.

"And why on earth did you run over there like that? Couldn't you see that he meant business? Good lord, Daddy, I was afraid he was going to hurt you."

There was no response from the passenger's side. The car dash glowed white with glass-focused sun rays.

Howard was standing on the mountain again, the sunlight boring into his straw hat. The pointer on the outdoor thermometer was stuck in his forehead. The chunking of Caterpillars was getting nearer.
"Get this old coot outta here!" a grinning Caterpillar said. Wilson pulled Howard's arm and his arm came off, floating freely and supporting his hand as it waved grandly over the surrounding landscape, showing the nearby counties.

Wilson went on, gathering courage while letting his words choose themselves, "And, for lord's sake, what did you mean by cussing that way? You let that man provoke you into swearing at him. Daddy, that sure didn't sound like you."

Howard was still turned toward the right pane, with his head on the cushioned rest. The gardens along the roadside were all drying up.

The okra and the martin bird droppings were getting harder to walk through, rough and fuzzy and smelling to high heaven, the tangles of the overgrown garden wrapping themselves around Howard's ankles. A sharp spade was chopping his foot, over and over again, but Howard felt no pain.

"But it was sort of funny," Wilson commented, with a half-smile tugging at the corners of his mouth. "He might not have heard what you said anyway. He said 'Good Day' like that was what you said…"

A weatherman on the car radio said the day was a warm one, as if no one could tell, no rain in sight. Howard raised a shaking hand to lower the sun visor.

An overhead sun in the Wal-Mart john was getting hotter and hotter. Howard was turning, turning in the blinding light as dust-covered creatures laughed at him, and the closed-up car took all his breath away. The largest yellow worm hovered over him with its shovel claw, laughing, laughing. But coming through and around it all, a hand cupped and reached down to lift him up, smiling, smiling.

"Daddy? Daddy?"
His father's wan yet peaceful look startled Wilson. Howard seemed to be sliding down in the seat. Wilson aimed the car for the hospital and broke the speed limit. Howard took long breaths of the cooling air, turned to the view that passed so quickly now, and smiled.

A LOTTA WOMAN

"You made it this far, Loretta. Don't you be backing out now."

The voice scolding Lottie was her own.

Although she still had to struggle to keep calm, Lottie was surprised at how easy it had been to become a traitor. She had stayed with her plan to this point, she told herself. Now if only the bus would move and she could finish escaping.

The wooden floor in her cold room had felt like pond ice. It was broad and worn and much-coated with pale chocolate paint like all the floors in the aging Kentucky farmhouse, even the ones that had some linoleum.

She had managed to finish packing her simple belongings in the dark, while keeping both feet on the steady floor board beside her bed. From there, she could, by twisting herself, reach the bottom level of the bureau. She had practiced in the daylight. Only that single plank was solid and stable. It must be stood on to keep from squeaking the other, weaker boards in the bedroom floor. As she pulled each bulbous knob, she was careful to balance the weight of each side of the drawer. When the heavy old wood lurched against itself, an awful squawk sometimes resulted.

"Hush that noise in there, Lottie Mae!" Papa would have growled, more like a loud whisper to keep from waking the others.

A few scuffing footsteps from the room he now shared with Doris, and he would have been at Lottie's side, seeing through her intentions. At twenty-nine, she was still beholden to her daddy and he was to her as well, with her still living in her childhood home but helping him, too, molding into her dead mother's place with chores and family care. Doris filled his bed, but he depended on Lottie to hold the disjointed family together. Both she and he knew it.

"Where you goin,' girl?" His tired eyes would have been confused, maybe hurt. Jerome Parmlee was not a harsh man, just a sad one, barely making it in a hard world, and here was his daughter leaving like a thief in the night. Lottie was glad she had not had to face him.

If she had known more about traveling, she might have put everything in one of Mama's soft pillowcases. It would surely have made less noise than the rustly brown paper grocery bag, she realized now.

But would they even let you on a bus with a pillowcase? Wouldn't it be hard to explain? Perhaps, though, not so difficult to explain a grocery sack folded over at the top. It could be thought to hold the proceeds of a shopping trip, or some vegetables that she, so obviously a country woman, was taking to a city cousin. Or even, as in Lottie's case, it suited for a change of clothes and the few necessary items for an overnight trip.

Not that overnight was all she was leaving for. Lottie's journey was only one way.

In the cool just-dawn of a summer morning that promised to be stifling before it was half over, not many people were at the bus station, and probably none for pleasure traveling. The dozen or so that waited for the lumbering Greyhound to pull in were dull and tired and already rumpled. Few seemed interested in their fellow travelers. Idle talk passed between some that acted like regulars, as though they had met here before.

"Reckon the trouble's finally finished over in Korea, just some big shots tying up loose ends now," announced a sage observer.

Somebody's boy was getting married when he could get home from over there.

Baseball was what they really talked about.

An unhappy fan groused, "This year sure oughter be better, or I'm gonna turn off the ray-dio for good. I'm a Saint Loo-is fan myself. " A large man with a pot-bellied stomach, he expanded his subject and got louder, "I bleeve that them coloreds is gon' ruin ballplaying anyhow."

From the seat beside him a freckled woman in a matching light denim skirt and shirtwaist blouse gave a disapproving snort and a furtive head jerk to remind him of the Negro janitor's presence. Her husband turned to her in a quick movement of anger, but turned back again quickly when he saw the man, and sat in a chastened silence from then on.

The thin black man in a faded uniform pushed a stringy gray dust mop the length of the hard tile floor and back, not looking up or around, widely skirting the few standing would-be passengers. With a quiet skill he managed to re-visit the spots he had so carefully missed, noticing when the standers moved just enough for them not to be bothered by him.

They all made Lottie nervous.

She had waited for the ticket cage to open, its occupant taking his time to roll his sleeves up evenly, clean his half-glasses, and adjust his visor before looking up for his first customer. By then Lottie was more a case of nerves than ever. She had moved her money from hand to hand, drying the sweat of first one and then the other.

Buying the ticket was a difficult task to make appear simple. Lottie blamed the earliness of the day for her stiff hands as she passed the money to the seated clerk. She tried to look casual as she pushed so many coins through a low opening in the black wire cage. The man's quick fingers expertly counted the few dollars of change with a rapid, energetic movement that was in contrast to the slow way he raised his head, looked at her steadily with no expression, then lowered his watery grey eyes and let her go, his hands working separately of his eyes the whole time.

She did not know what she would have said if he had tried to make conversation. What if he had remarked on the combination of small bills and coins that she had been collecting so long? Even though Lottie had not traveled herself, she knew something of others who pulled out well-worn checkbooks, or at the very least laid down large-denomination bills.

The clerk did not seem to mind, though. With a practiced rhythm he filled small oblong spaces in a wooden drawer, as if the odd assortment were usual and even welcome.

Now seated on the bus as it idled beside the others in the lot, Lottie was amazed at her progress so far, but terrified too. She felt lightheaded and wobbly, in part due to the strangeness of the weak dome light and to the constant movement of people on the platform just under the window and onto the bus itself.

She had almost forgotten the other reason for her discomfort. Her lightheadedness gave way to nausea, and Lottie panicked. When she had slipped out of the house she had been so careful to put on her housecoat and to hold the sack under it close to her fully clothed body. If anyone woke or happened to be coming from the outhouse, where she was pretending to go, she had planned to clutch herself and the sack around her middle as if to indicate a need to go quickly, with no time to answer questions.

No such questioning person had materialized, and Lottie still marveled at the freedom with which she had moved down the path, behind the barn, and out onto the road, her housecoat by that time stowed in the paper sack with her few other clothes.

But she had not actually made a trip to the outhouse.

All but paralyzed by uncertainty, Lottie wondered if she should get up and go back into the bus station to use the restroom before the bus was to pull out. Others were doing that, or seeing someone to speak to, or having a last cigarette, serenely waiting to board, and none of them worrying about the vehicle leaving. For Lottie, however, the thought was terrifying, and she could no more move from the bus than take wings and fly. She would put off her need by force of will.

She was relieved to have another passenger, a pleasant and not too neat older woman, her severe bun of iron gray hair lashed in place with bobby pins, sit down beside her. It took Lottie's attention off her bladder as the bus began to move, and she silently congratulated herself for not feeling uncomfortable with this stranger.

Lottie's seatmate was blithely concerned with her own matters and carried on such a non-stop, gossipy line of talk that Lottie did not feel she had to respond, except to smile and agree or mumble some noncommittal responses to unimportant questions.

"You ever see such a bunch of women with their hair bobbed off?" Lola Stadler had inquired and then answered herself instantly, "I believe it's wrong by the Bible, but I ain't one to tell other people what to do."

And she had a keen sense of observation that, thankfully, seemed to omit Lottie. "That there funny-looking boy with that couple, don't you think there's somethin' furrin about him?" Again the wise Lola replied to her own question, "I think mebbe he's one of them war orphans. I bet his folks was Jews or somebody and got killed…"

It was from Mrs. Stadler that Loretta learned of the restroom on the bus.

"These nice new buses have 'em," she said, "and they're real small, but they work just like a real one."

Lottie could not have told her that her "real" one had a wooden plank with two holes in it. When the older woman returned from the toilet herself, Lottie had built up her courage and she stood up just as her seat partner returned. Again pleased with herself on the smoothness of a plan carried out, she remarked that she was about to go anyway and she thought she'd just get up and keep Mrs. Stadler from having to move for her.

Lottie's fear that the woman would think her odd for carrying a grocery sack to the restroom was unfounded, too. Her squirrelly chatter kept her blissfully unconcerned over any of Lottie's actions. Lottie really thought that if she had pulled a gun out of the bag, or even a snake, Mrs. Stadler would have gone on telling her about the neighbor lady back home who had the son whose oldest girl worked at the hospital in Bowling Green and had seen all manner of lord knows what that came into that place, and so on.

Now back in her seat, what bothered Lottie most was the result of having stuffed herself with her food while in the bus restroom. It had been like being in the outhouse because of the lingering smells. That, combined with the haste of swallowing cornbread without a washing-down liquid, had left her very uncomfortable. At home she would have had milk, at least, or buttermilk. The water from the tiny faucet had been her only choice. What with leaning her head sideways in the lavatory and gulping at the trickle, she had almost choked on the rough cornmeal texture.

For a moment she had feared she would have one of those severe spells that her great-uncle Jerney had fought several times when cornbread hung in his throat. They nearly sent him into a seizure before the liquid he should have drunk in the first place finally made it to the offended throat area.

Soon her discomfort eased, however, and Lottie began to drowse, with the old woman's drone providing a peaceful background. With her head laid back at an angle against the seat so she could see out the window, Lottie locked her fingers behind the sack. Now emptied of the cornbread at least, the smoothed-out paper was almost flat against her belly. Her shoes were wedged firmly and evenly against the bottom of the empty seat in front of her, and her soft, flabby arm felt comfortable against the cool bus wall.

The very modern air conditioning system on the vehicle was producing a relaxing hum, and the refrigerated air it blew made her feel sleepy. But of course she could not allow herself to fall asleep. Everything was behind, but much was ahead, too.

Colors and shapes of the countryside rushed by in such varying detail that Lottie often found her eyes following a scene and then starting with another and then another, so that she was soon feeling dizzy again. She made herself concentrate on thinking about her new life.

In the right pocket of her thin cotton sweater was the picture. She did not want to get it out and have to explain it to Mrs. Stadler. But it felt good just to touch the pocket, to feel the shape of the small square safe inside. Like a secret. Yes, a secret she had kept well. From Papa and all the others.

Guilt started to get the best of Lottie. They would be getting up now. Probably somebody had already been to the outhouse and had come back in and piled up among the quilts again, burrowing in until the coffee smell would reach him, the coffee that would not be made this day, as least not by Lottie. Jerney, no doubt, would be that early one. He used the covered pot by his bed at night, but he often was the first to go to the weathered outbuilding in the morning, a hard trip in any season because of his creeping years and arthritis. Had he noticed that Lottie was gone? Probably not. His mind was often still on the mountain where he and his brothers and sisters, all long dead, had been children, and he was still a child to this day. He would only notice when he got hungry and Lottie was not there to feed and pet him.

"Where you go?" he would demand when she had been only a few minutes away.

"Lott? Don' leave me," he had blubbered on more than one occasion when she had done nothing more than go outside and hang clothes.

Lottie's eyes started with tears and she turned again toward the bus window to hide them. The heaving, gearing sounds of the large vehicle covered the snuffle she almost let go. She would have to think that the others would be good to Jerney.

The bus lurched into its first destination, just a pickup at a small grocery store for some mail and sometimes a local who would ride standing up by the driver and talk and get off only a few miles down the road. The practice was normal. It was a system that worked to get folks from one place to another. It was logical, no need to waste the chance. Lottie still envied the natural ease with which people accomplished these simple moves that moved their lives onward. But she had done it, too, hadn't she—just getting up and getting out and getting on this bus and going—oh, Lord, what had she done?

Lottie wanted to scream and run off the bus at the stop but was rooted to the metal grid beneath her feet. As the door screeched open and the driver got off to stretch his long legs and have a smoke with the lady who ran

Wanetta's Food Stop, Lottie saw her chance but had no feet to carry her. The casual interlude would have been the perfect opportunity for her to escape the bus and start walking back home, unnoticed and uncared about by anyone. Too soon the tall, laughing busman flung the last of his cigarette down and ground it with his shoe. He took the steps with one leap and fell into the seat refreshed, immediately setting his machine in motion. Lottie told herself it was his fault, his being in such a hurry, that she did not manage to get off in time.

The landscape had already become unfamiliar. The humble houses and simple farms of her region of Kentucky had given way to neater, finer homes and estates lined with the long stone walls and wood fencing common to Bluegrass horse country. Roads were wider, with more cars and few walkers, and definitely no horses. Oh, there were certainly horses, but of the kept, rich kind, to be seen within the white-fenced areas of the farms that the bus now passed, with names that read like the Courier-Journal on Derby Day.

The horses that Lottie did not see were ones with names like Dickey and Bonnie, Papa's work team that pulled the plow on weekdays and stood dozing outside the barn on Sundays. Lottie could not remember Dickey and Bonnie pulling a buggy as Papa had talked about them doing in the older days, but sometimes still they hauled a wagon out to the sorghum mill and back. She could not imagine the slow, plodding giants making their way on these hard roads where some people must drive up to nearly fifty miles an hour.

Maybe somebody had combed Jerney's hair for him. And washed the oatmeal off his stubbly old gray face.

She forced the guilt and tears back again. Mrs. Stadler was sleeping and the day was waning. The afternoon had indeed become hot, and the air conditioning was working hard. It was a good time to look at the picture. Lottie slipped the small color photograph out and held it to the window. The form was in her memory, so that, if she had been an artist, she had believed she would have been able to trace it and color it to perfection. But now she stared at it and saw it new again.

Gerald. The brown wavy hair, the strong jaw, the easy smile and the eyes. Those laughing eyes. The eyes were crinkled almost shut with the smile. But his eyes were—what color? She squinted and blamed the dying day, realizing that she did not know the color of his eyes. Panic seized her again, and her stomach did a flip. She was cold anyway from the cooled air, but a chill took hold of her as she began to fear that she was holding a picture of a complete stranger.

Lottie shoved the picture quickly down into the worn cardigan's pocket and pulled the thin garment around her, moving down into the seat, seeking a safe place. Sleep would finally come as she rode through the night, come and go as would Lottie's thoughts, rock and weave and pitch and roll until the light came again.

Vera wanted to be a movie star. She told everybody. They just didn't take her seriously. She secretly planned to run away someday and never be heard from again until they all went down to the Astor Cinema in Bowling Green and saw her up there with that good-looking young Rock Hudson. She would maybe wait until she was fifteen, but then again maybe she couldn't stand it. But she would show everybody. So it made Vera furious when she found out that Lottie, big old dumb ugly fat Lottie, had run off first, had made everybody pay attention to her, had stolen Vera's thunder. Now all she could ever be if she ran off was another one, a second one, just like her dumb old fat old ugly step-sister Lottie. She hated her and hoped she was dead somewhere.

Vera's mother Doris found the note. She was not much older than her husband's daughter Loretta and liked her in a way, but she had never been close to her, and she was afraid Jerome would blame her for not seeing it coming.

He didn't say anything, though. He just listened to the note, put his coffee cup down, pulled on his baseball cap, and went out to the truck. The rough motor coughed a little, then started, and carried him away to the grimy building that pretended to be a sportsman's lodge. At night, after a day of cold beer, he came home and slept in his clothes on the living room couch. He didn't talk about Lottie at all.

Shellie was too young to absorb it all, but he missed Lottie. She was the one who fixed him something to eat after school, when Mama was getting her hair done or was on the phone, and although she didn't talk much about herself, Lottie liked to hear about what had happened to him on the playground or in the cafeteria with the other second graders.

And she had gone to school with him that day when the other children had their parents there. Mama was sick, she said, and got mad at him for asking her to go. She shut herself in the bedroom and stayed there. Daddy never went to anything at school. In the days when Lottie was growing up, Mary Ann had handled all that. Being a father again, even with a boy this time, Jerome did not see any reason to start doing what was uncomfortable for him. It was a woman's place.

But Lottie had quietly whispered to Shellie, and had met him in the lunchroom with the other families. He was happy. She was prettier than anybody's mother that was there, with her Sunday meeting dress on, and Shellie never let on that she wasn't his mother. She even talked to the teachers and the school workers, stood right there and made talk like Mama would never have done.

She had gone a couple of times after that, too, for a special awards day and a holiday program, all without any of the rest of the family knowing. They had shared a special secret from the rest of the family, and now she was gone. Shellie would never tell the others how much he missed her. They would really still have a secret that way.

Jerney was lost as always, but more pitiful than usual. He wore his nightclothes all day and peed in his drawers and cried when he slept. Vera said he needed to go to a home.

"He IS home," Jerome made clear. Jerome cleaned Jerney up a little and cut his long, dirty fingernails. Jerney still cried but took to following his nephew Jerome around when he was home, and Jerome let him.

Lottie straightened herself up the best that she could at each station, in each succeeding restroom. For one who had previously had next to no experience with modern facilities, she was becoming a great judge of washrooms.

Certain mirrors and soap dishes and faucets were superior to others, she had decided, and she hoped that the bathroom would be nice wherever she ended up. Now a bath itself was what she missed. She longed for the big old clawfoot tub on the closed-in back porch, with several teakettles of heated water and a fresh bar of berry-scented lye soap, although she knew she should consider it all primitive now that she was a woman of the world. She had struggled to continue a fairly thorough ongoing clean-up, though, and was as fresh as she could manage in her traveling life.

Leaving the last bus, Lottie was asked by the porter at the large Lexington station about her suitcases. She had stuffed her personal belongings, even the other brassiere and an extra pair of hosiery, into the pockets of her dress's gathered skirt and into her mother's old purse, so that the paper grocery sack had been done away with. Lottie indicated that a traveling companion had already gotten the luggage, thanks anyway, and left the porter standing at the gaping hole in the side of the bus. Holding herself in as dignified a manner as possible, she walked away quickly, as if to catch up with her companion.

Once up to the bus station platform, Lottie straightened her flowered rayon dress and untwisted the belt that had crawled halfway up to her bosom. She stopped at a bench at the entrance and wilted heavily onto it. Soon she would begin her life, but she did not feel hopeful or happy, just confused and lost.

The photo of Gerald had become even more the picture of a stranger. She did not even want to look at it again. Her sweater with its pocket secret was now best used as a cushion between her backside and the hard slats.

Lottie's feet were swollen in the cheap vinyl flats she had worn day and night now. She had languished in stuffy, dirty bus stations for hours at a stretch to connect with the next bus and the next one in the snaking journey. Her behind was sore from sitting on rough wooden pews and rusting metal frames with cracked green cushions that had stuck to her through her thin dress and slip. Her hair had perspiration in it and there were no hairpins to tame it, so it hung limp but threatened to start going its own way soon. A young boy just off the bus with his mother whispered to his sister and they both pointed at Lottie and laughed at her. Lottie felt hungry and sick.

A heavy, sweating man stood near where Lottie sat. She was sure her stomach would turn over if she had to endure any more body smells, as the buses had been resplendent with them. She turned away to change the air flow, but became aware that she was being watched.

"Loretta?"

It almost had sounded like her name. The bus's roar had deafened her, and the abrupt, harsh sounds of the city assaulted her ears and confused her.

"Loretta, is that you?"

Reluctantly she looked up and saw the jaw and the hair and something of the smile and the no-color eyes, but none of it added up. They were individually all there but did not go together. They were contained in the wrong body of the heavy, sweaty man. This person was surely not Gerald. Please, not Gerald.

His look was uncertain. She was so lost in her disappointment that it took her a moment to answer him.

"Gerald?" She squinted up at his large shape that blocked out the sun. "Yes, it's me...Lottie. How...how are you?" It was nothing to say, but she could excuse staring at him because they were holding a conversation.

"Oh, fine, I'm fine..." The conversation sputtered and all but died.

Her turn, but she passed.

"So, how was the trip?" He was valiant if anything, and polite, but obviously struggling.

"Fine, uh, fine..." It was getting worse, not better.

He took some deep breaths. She was afraid to.

"So, you want to go get something to eat?" he offered, along with his hand to help her up.

Lottie gawked up at him and found herself allowing him to lift her up to his height. But she was evidently still sitting. He was still a head and more taller than she was. She wondered how photographs could be so deceiving. In the small, square head and shoulders picture he had been clean and neat and not so bulky. And somehow she had concluded he would be just the perfect height for her to lift her perfectly made-up lips to his to receive a perfect, mint-smelling kiss.

As though a mirror had been whirled to show its glassy surface to her, Lottie suddenly saw what Gerald's struggle might be about. She remembered the two children's reaction and became painfully aware of her own appearance. The unruliness of her hair and her overall unkempt look came clearly into her view and drove away all judgments of Gerald. She knew she was relatively clean, but she had forgotten all about her overweight body.

Whatever had possessed her to come here and meet him after this brief communication through friends? The picture that she had sent to him was several years and many pounds earlier, and taken on one of those unusual days when the light was just right and flattered her. She could see why he looked like someone who was picking up a damaged shipment at the catalog store.

"Oh, I had lunch," Lottie managed. "There were machines in the last station…" She tried to stop staring.

Gerald shifted his weight to another foot.

"Well, uh, I thought you, I thought you would be, you know, hungry…" He had only this one offer prepared.

She finally agreed, then, if only to put him out of his misery. They walked down a grainy concrete sidewalk past a furniture store and some small, boarded-up shops. When it came time to enter a restaurant, Gerald held a heavy outer door open with his hand high up on the facing and with her having to pass through under his armpit. She instinctively stopped her breathing and passed under, but when she breathed again, there was no smell. She was glad. Maybe Gerald was not smelly after all.

The small restaurant had a lobby that was entered by this pair of glass doors and then opened through two more into the dining area. Two people inside were starting to come out. As Lottie and Gerald approached the inner doors, she could see the couple coming from inside toward the second set of doors. The man reached high to open the door for the lady. He was tall and handsome, a regular football hero, and the woman was short and fluffy, but small beside the man. She looked as though she could be tucked away under his arm. But when the second doors opened, the other couple was gone. They had disappeared.

Gerald ordered confidently, for both of them, even what to drink without asking her. Lottie was impressed by that for some reason. It was as though he read her tiredness and was trying to help. She looked up with surprise when the cute blond waitress took his order with a flirt in her voice. When he got up to move his chair in toward the table better, Lottie saw the football player again. It was Gerald. Their own reflection as a couple had greeted her in the lobby.

Lottie wanted to hide, but there was nowhere to go. Here she was with this stranger, not a bad-looking stranger after all, and she knew she looked awful. Lotta Lottie, the other children had teased. A whole lotta Lottie. And she still was. So she did what she did best. Lottie ate silently but quickly.

Gerald managed to swallow his butterbeans but had a big lump in his throat that had nothing to do with food.

He had waited for this day for weeks. The deal had begun when Stan, his best and sometimes worst friend, teased him about a date set-up. He said that his wife Sherie, who worked for the state and had to travel around, had been at a school conference where the parents were supposed to come, and that a pleasant woman about Gerald's age was there to help with her younger half-brother. She had even let herself pass as his mother. Who knows what kind of problems there were in that home? And wouldn't Gerald like to know a young woman like that?

Stan and Sherie had played the right card. Gerald had a soft heart.

The only trouble was what Gerald thought of himself. He didn't let himself get off as easily as he did other people, especially nice ladies and little kids. He was big and graceless, good at work and always dependable, but no prize. Stan had wrestled a high-school picture away from him and sent it to Lottie, and Sherie had gotten a picture of her and brought it to him. Gerald had fallen right away.

Letters, short notes really, were passed between the two with the aid of Stan and Sherie. Sherie still had her doubts about Lottie's home situation and did not want to pry, but especially did not want to do anything to harm the children who might be there. She did not know that the arrangement that the two had made in the most recent letter could possibly separate Lottie from little Shellie, perhaps forever.

Now, Gerald and Lottie had met each other. The first impression was not good. Gerald knew that probably this relationship was now destined to die a-borning.

Sometimes people do exaggerate their good qualities or disguise their faults, but they are bound to be found out, Gerald decided. This was a good example. He just had to decide on the most careful way to get out of an unfortunate situation.

"Gerald?" a soft voice came from somewhere about his shoulder. "Gerald?"

He looked down at the short woman across the table from him. Her gray eyes were kind, he decided. Well, knowing about the little brother made that an easy guess, of course.

"Gerald, I suppose you could say that today has been sort of…surprising," she said delicately.

He breathed a little easier. She did understand. No harm had been intended. He nodded dumbly and tried to smile to relieve her.

Smiling back, Lottie seemed to be reluctant to be the one to end the conversation and the unborn relationship. Gerald knew he had to say something, too.

"You are real nice," he amazed himself at saying, "and I'm so sorry…" He floundered and did not finish.

His unfinished apology hung in the air amid the restaurant sounds. Easy conversations and laughter mingled with kitchen noises and provided a disinterested backdrop for their improbable scene. No one would notice or care if one or both got up and left the table now, for good.

She confounded him by seeming to want to continue talking.

"The…the lunch was thoughtful. I want to thank you…" she managed.

She who was so much a woman, a lot of woman if he ever saw one, was missing a perfect opportunity to leave, thought Gerald. Surely such a woman would rush to get away from this oaf of a man, awkward and inelegant, who had misrepresented his appearance in a hopelessly outdated photograph.

He was still sitting there, thought Lottie, not moving as any idiot should have been, to get away from the fat, dumpy woman with the hair beginning to frizz, who was obviously in high school when her picture was made.

Instead, thought Gerald, she still sat there with her soft little curls and those pretty gray eyes, looking like a doll. From the time he had seen her on the bench at the station, he had been afraid she would get away. And here she was, staying.

Now he stood tall, offering her his hand. They both smiled awkwardly as they made ready to leave the restaurant together. What a man, thought Lottie, his handsome hulk so male and reassuring, his gentle manner so appealing to a woman. Could it be—he liked her?

Somewhere a couple of streets over, a Greyhound shifted gears and roared its departure. Lottie had wondered if she would ever go home again, and now she knew she would. However, things would be different. Jerney and Shellie would cling to her and cry, but they would be happy. Lottie and her man would be coming to get them both and have them come visit in the city.

WILD ONIONS

A few degrees of warming sunshine meant he had no more excuses. Bill prepared to do battle with the emerging season.

The March ground, still hard and cold, would rebuke any planting yet. It would allow only the dragging out of last fall's leaves, clumped nasty and dark behind the cobbled rocks that surrounded Emily's flower garden. Other leaves, brittle and raspy, were held by skeletons of overgrown bushes and dry vines. With the rusted tines of a rake Bill dug at the trapped brown curls and cursed the stubbornness of their captors.

Flower gardening was a waste of time as far as Bill was concerned. But Emily was known for just about the prettiest displays around. He needed now, while it was still early, to clean up this one spot for her at least, to relieve it of its strangled look. Then, he allowed, whatever plants of the decent variety that were willing to present themselves could come forth with a tad more ease.

A few minutes more, however, and he felt ready to throw down the rake and concede the fight. He consigned the rangy bed to a list of things he would mow down first thing when it was warm enough.

Please, Billy, don't cut down my buttercups...they'll be blooming soon...and the butterfly bush—just trim it low so it'll come back.

Her voice came to him clear as real, and he stood listening amid the ragged display.

It was a shame, this dead and tangled place. Emily's flowers were noticed. Some showed up at all different seasons and shifted around, making a community of their own, sharing and bartering and moving their goods here and there. The perpetual yearly production was spontaneous, accomplished with long-ago plantings of perennials, mixed with wild flowers that Emily had let stand where they surprised.

In the bare branches a brisk wind rattled their caught leaves and its cold went straight through Bill's much-washed denim overalls and a double layer of shirts.

No namer of blooming things, with the exception of fruit trees in spring or squash blossoms in summer, Bill did not have words for many plants, especially those awakening at his feet. The daffodils or buttercups were easy enough, as several of their yellow crowns were already showing. Raking had beheaded some of them, and others were revealed as the leaves left. He knew that these hiding ones would be blooming also, although still covered with debris or snow.

Early spring in Kentucky, he observed, is time for fools to be out. Pretty in its own way, yes, but cold and dangerous, too.

The scared little flowers show up, all wobbly and pale. And sure enough, along comes a late snow. Out of the north it prowls, looking for something getting ready to stand out in the open and just be pretty. Then they barely peek out, their creamy trumpets fragile and feathery, and it covers them over with its white freeze. But—fool things—they dare to bloom and maybe die when it would be better to just lie low and wait to have their color.

He called them buttercups mostly, not daffodils. He wanted them to have strength and bright color and tell the snow to go straight to, well, a word Emily wouldn't approve. Butter was a good word, though, a strong word, solid like a patted, cool cake of it, sunny like promises. Buttercups should be allowed to glow, to stand and reach tall for the spring sun, glorying in the golden days.

Bill had more words, however, and for sure ones Emily wouldn't allow, for the wild onions that cropped up wherever they wished, inside and outside the rock-rimmed circle. Even with gloves on, he hated to pull at the tight sprocks. They would resist his tug and leave their pungent scent in the air and on his gloves' palms. Their many-knotted roots had developed already. No way to get rid of wild onions—they were too strong and pulled the earth out with them when they came and would always come back, even if dug out. Later in the summer, they would finally go to seed on their own schedule, some with tough bulb heads to continue their kind when they had fallen to the earth.

Wild onions were to be admired after all, Bill admitted grudgingly. Tough and strong, they would endure despite human efforts to dislodge them.

Whatever in the great plan of creation kept them vigorous and unyielding, smelling like victory itself, did not also make them beautiful or desirable. But their survival did not depend upon any judgment of their worth as decided by a man with a rake. Bill would leave them alone in their hardiness and spend his efforts where they would count, on less worthy opponents like brittle branches and rotting leaves.

Stiffly bending to retrieve the U.K. Wildcats cap that had fallen into some leafy trash, Bill ran a bony hand through his hair and jammed the sweat-rimmed khaki more firmly onto his head. In the past the plastic band that decided his skull size would have wedged a ring around his full hair, but now it hit the ever-larger thinning area on the crown of his scalp so that a bald spot shone through the hole at the cap's back. He had to lift his cap by its bill again and make his long hair from the front and sides cover the emptiness in the back.

His mane was stringy and he had let it grow too long. With spring and summer would come more haircuts, but for now he welcomed the extra covering and the feel of the cap holding the hair down. Although becoming practiced at removing old growth here in the yard, he would wait to clean himself up. He had no promise, after all, of a recurring crop of hair waiting for the cleared space on his pate.

Because of its name, Bill only recognized one other plant—euonymus, a proliferate bush with branches that spiraled their way here and there, forming wound-up messes that caught more oak leaves.

Emily had said something about its auspicious, favorable name with that "eu"on it—*good, happy,* like *euphoria* and *euphemism*, she had rattled on, English teacher talk. Bill presently felt anything but favorable toward the growth as he struggled with its snarls. *You-onymus, no, just you go on and go away and be your cheerful, aggravating self in somebody else's garden.*

Dry and wan now at the end of winter, the plant still was aggressive. Edged with white, the euonymus leaves were small and evenly spaced on both sides of long, flexible tendrils that grew and grew and took root wherever they touched the ground.

One especially exasperating trailer currently seemed to enjoy impeding his work. It flung itself somehow into every rake's worth of dead leaves, causing Bill to have to reach over and un-catch it. On several occasions he took hold of the vine and wound it around an old spray-painted water pump in the center of the ten-foot diameter garden.

It would quickly unwind itself and fall with a jerk onto his raked pile, taunting him like a cat, Bill decided. Just like a pesky little tom he and Emily had once kept. Always jumping into and out of your laundry or other work

Look, Bill! Shhh—Tiger is in the clothes basket on top of your jeans. He won't hurt anything, no worse than the dog hairs you have all over you from Krispy!

And look! look! how he's winding up his rear end to jump out on something!

The butterfly bush must be this one, he reasoned. Of some size and height, it might be the anchor of the garden spot, just important enough for her to single out for special care. In this season it was only a bony cluster of sticks reaching to six feet or more. With a red-handled pruning tool drawn from a pocket of the overalls, he started trimming at chest level.

"I saw you trying to get rid of them earlier. It'll never work that way," a woman's voice announced, and Bill followed the musical sound to its speaker. His neighbor Gloria Sevetts was stepping carefully over the mole-tunneled sod in her small pink canvas sneakers, picking her way on the more solid, grassy parts. Nearing his pitiful work site, she smiled and extended a hand wearing one very feminine gardening glove and carrying a coffee can with some liquid in it. Gloria waved a delicate artist's brush like a tiny baton with the other gloved hand.

Bill was bewildered by her reference, thinking at first that she meant his current project, the butterfly bush stalks. Then, he realized even as his mind was confused a bit more by the blue-jeaned legs that carried her toward him, she must be talking about the wild onions. She would have been watching him earlier, when he had tried to pull them loose and then had given up. It was somehow a nice feeling that she had looked and cared about his struggles.

"Here," she declared with authority, "this is what you need. It's weed killer, and all you have to do is brush it on the blades with this little paint brush, see, and those old onions will just dry right up and die."

Out of breath with her rush to give the helpful advice and to reach Bill before he decided to tug any more at the stubborn onion clumps, Gloria had quit watching for the last of the soft mole runs and nearly lost her balance.

Bill dropped the snippers and deftly caught the woman's liquid offering before it could kill half the yard, while also making a decent grab for her slender elbow, keeping her from spilling as well. He was surprised and proud he could move so fast, considering his sixty-eight-year-old bones and the eternal presence of his friend "Arthur"—his and Emily's joking name for unamusing arthritis pain.

And when Gloria lurched against him, her rescuer, he felt a long-forgotten thrill. The presence of a woman's vital body in his arms once again was shockingly familiar. It jarred his composure and he sounded foolish, without dignity, as he spoke.

"Whoa, there," he chuckled, "you're gonna end up down in Mister Mole's ditch if you don't watch out. These doggoned varmints have got the yard so worked up, and then this wet spring with all the rain, well, you might sink down and we'd never see you again."

They both laughed, and without stepping away he twisted around and set the weed dope in a safe spot just inside the ring of rocks, then turned to her again, this time realizing how close they were standing to each other. He could smell the shower-freshness of her, mingled with some kind of perfume or powder. For a sixty-something, a silvering blonde with short, soft curls, she was pretty and fixed herself up nice, he observed.

It was Bill Stewart's turn to be dizzy.

He managed to croak out, "I'm not much of a flower gardener, you see." Then before he knew it, he added, "That's Emily's department. She's the one who gets out here..." Any more caught in his throat.

In the silence Gloria stared for a minute, then touched

his arm with her fancy glove. Her hand lingered and she stroked his flannel shirt, the muscle and bone beneath coming alive with her gentle kneading. Her upturned soft grey eyes were not leaving his face, but searching for his eyes, letting the moment speak for itself. She was available for his needs. To talk, perhaps.

Bill politely let her hand caress his stiffened forearm, but did not dare to look down into her eyes. Feigning deafness or unawareness, he casually moved away as soon as her sympathetic clutch released slightly.

With more interest than necessary, he carefully inspected the thin brush and the can of deadly solution. If it had a vile smell, he could not say, even with it directly under his nostrils. They were too full of some wonderful woman-scent, working its way into his brain and threatening to control his body as well.

"But, I thank you," he said with inordinate cheer, "and I'm glad to get something to try to get rid of these here rascals. They smell up a place awful."

Plunging on with more separating words, he remarked as if the thought had suddenly occurred, "Sure is a cold spring, don't you think? But it's turnin,' I reckon, it's turnin.' You know what they say, 'When winter comes, can spring be far behind...'"

Bill could hear himself nearly shouting at the petite woman only inches from him. Would his loudness make their conversation public, not private? Could he be heard in the house?

He watched the floral patterned hands withdraw in gentle embarrassment. A rush of words he could not say forced their way to his lips and stopped. He had hurt her feelings but it could not be helped. Emily was just inside.

After Gloria, in her short white jacket and nice-fitting jeans, had disappeared from his lingering watch around the garage and back to her house, Bill set at the cleaning project once more.

His ruffled thoughts made for distraction. Forgetting that he had more recently been clipping the dry butterfly bush stalks, he grabbed the rake again and went after some drying debris where he had scooped up wet leaves earlier. Even as he wielded the tool, however, he remembered his lost routine and barely scraped at the littered ground, intending to change course after this one pass with the teeth. But the euonymus creeper caught him.

It flung itself as before into the area he was working. There were fewer massed leaves for the roping tendril to play in, so it resorted to entangling his nearly empty rake. Bill angrily whapped the ground to loosen the plant's hold, but the ensuing dance he had with the waving vine did no good and made him more angry. The euonymus seemed to be delighting in the ride. Bill jerked the vine with a vengeance, yet it only rolled out more and more length, like a cowboy's rope. Was there no end to this plant's determination? Why did it latch onto him?

Was not the wind a more worthy companion, with no list of things to do or limited time to do them?

But maybe the tomcat vine, he recalled having naming it, maybe it just needed a lively little girl-cat vine, even a pretty, powdered-smelling sixty-year-old girl...Brought up short by his sudden longing and the shame of it, Bill jerked the vine again more sharply, this time drawing its attention as he punished its wantonness. It fell to the ground in disarray, a cowering coil that all but whimpered.

Betty Wills was standing on the Stewarts' back porch, her arms crossing her ample belly. The old man had finally noticed her there. A frown visible to Bill half a yard away indicated her displeasure at having had to overstay her promised time because the woman's husband had been fiddling with that ugly old rock bed — and no doubt enjoying the company of a neighbor lady in a man-catching getup, way too fancy for a stroll in a cold March yard. Betty had seen but would not say anything about it. She just wanted her pay and to get home before "Days" came on. Roman and Marlena were maybe about to get back together.

"Sorry," Bill called to her as he closed the clippers and sloughed off his jersey gloves. He shoved everything into his overall pockets as he stumbled over the rock edge and strode quickly toward the house.

Bounding up the porch steps, he tried to make it better. "Us old men can't remember anything. I clean forgot the time," he joked to her unsmiling face.

With an exaggerated air of regret for his inattention, he held the back door open with a bow and a sweeping gesture for Betty to enter and get her purse. He was overdoing the courtesy, he knew, but women who did this work were hard to get and keep. Besides, she was honest and needed the money, and would get snapped up by somebody else if she left Bill and Emily. He could kiss a little...well, looking at Betty's wide rear as she hurried in and snatched up her shoulder bag and UK jacket...maybe, if necessary, a LOT of butt to keep her coming for her shift.

The putrid smell reached him in a wave, taking his breath of a sudden as he hurried to scribble Mrs. Wills's check.

Stopping his nose as much as possible without clamping it with his fingers, Bill managed to ease the woman on her way with a continuing mumbled apology, noting that Betty Wills herself did not even flinch at the odor. He assumed this was because she knew it was out of her province, that the accident had occurred after her watch was officially over, and he had delayed her actual leaving due to his tardiness.

When he closed the front door behind her, though, and opened the bedroom door, he rushed to cover his nose and wipe his smarting eyes, having discovered that the soiling must have happened much earlier. It was an abundant amount and indescribably foul. Was Mrs. Wills so cold that she was determined to punish him even if it meant temporarily enduring the stink herself? But then, she was on the back porch for a while, he recalled, maybe longer than he knew. His excuses for her were running thin, however.

Driven by anger and frustration, Bill turned the large air cleaner on high, hoisted the dusty blinds to the top, and flung open a window, the one toward the lonely flower bed.

Hurriedly gathering mops and towels and garbage bags, with strong disinfectant and hot water he attacked the bowel movement that covered the bed and the floor beside it.

Nearly gagging, he nevertheless moved smoothly due to much experience, holding and lifting Emily above and out of the ruin that had escaped her body. This was accomplished deftly, as Bill had long practice. Her gaunt, nearly lifeless body was now only a few pounds and easy to heft, and he grasped her with one rock-a-bye arm that carried her in infant fashion. Then he discovered the matted filth that caked the bottom of her nightgown. His hand had reached directly into it.

He damned the negligent Betty Wills, who clearly had left it all for him for some spiteful purpose. She of no emotion had evidently been making her escape at the door just now with what she had decided to be her last check. Bill agreed fervently that it would be her last indeed.

With automatic movements born of necessity, Bill pulled the gown off the rag doll who was his bride, wadded and hurled the stained ball across the room.

"Wuh?" came the strangled, weak voice, from a mouth he had thought never to hear speak again.

The ravaged remains of what had been Emily's lovely face were lit by the cold March sky that filled her open window. She was staring out toward the shorn garden spot, at some world she had left long ago, with a hint of eagerness and recognition that made Bill the saddest he could ever feel. It was easier having her sleep or sit with no awareness as she had for months now. This glimpse of what was lost wrenched his gut more than the fecal odor had done.

He wept for her then, for her and for him, his nose lowered into her coarse hair, short cut for invalid care. He breathed deeply, filling his lungs with the sourness, inhaling the stench and the staleness, holding her tightly to him.

Her face was still toward the window, though she did not see or respond past the first half-question. She was limp as usual in his arms, but he held her tightly.

His tears wet her dry, flaked scalp and his nostrils leaked into the sour strands of the hair that had been bright and beautiful.

Outside in Emily's garden, the can knocked over by Bill's foot had completed its watering, too. The killing poison had drained through the curled-up pile of once playful euonymus, innocent and unaware that its fate was now sealed. The tomcat vine would die.

But the wild onions were not touched. Their scent was stronger than ever.

MIRROR, MIRROR

Mirrors do not lie, but it might be nice if they would just tell some face-saving falsehoods once in a while. Margaret's mirror needed a lesson in finesse, she decided. Its harsh opinion had been delivered, no holds barred, first thing on a Monday morning.

"What's wrong with you? You look dreadful!" the silvery surface had whispered, its tone more critical than helpful.

Not that Miss Margaret Denton was in the habit of speaking to her furniture, but neither did she intend to entertain its appraisal of her physical qualities. After a few long seconds of shocked silence, Margaret felt a reasonable anger rising. Had she spoken aloud to this wooden coat and hat rack, she would have liked to say, "Who cares what you think?"

In the ornate hall tree the mirror maintained its unpleasant judgment, however, and Margaret did not really need to challenge the question. Her own eyes proved the truthfulness of the mirror's criticism. The woman in the looking glass was tall and gaunt, with a slackness of early middle age becoming quite noticeable in her face. Sprigs of wayward curls went their own way.

Margaret did not ordinarily set much store by her appearance, and had only meant to check for a crisp, efficient look. Pausing at the mirror on her habitual morning trek from back to front of her home to make sure all was exactly as it should be, she had patted her pinned hair and brushed the faded but practical housedress. Her actions, streamlined and automatic, had been intended today, as always, simply to establish a workaday neatness. Superficial beauty was not a thing of importance. In her image and in her life, she valued evenness, and it was all she had expected from the daily glance.

This morning, however, with no warning, the quiet routine had been altered by the mirror's rude comment. Whether she wanted to admit it or not, Margaret indeed did not see what she had expected. The neat, reasonably handsome, relatively youngish woman that she had seen all other mornings was missing. In her place was an apparition, with mortality registering in her flesh. Margaret recognized her forty-year-old self and slumped. Her exhaled sigh concluded with a weak trembling, and she hurried to sit down at the kitchen table.

Elbows on ancient, much-washed oilcloth, Margaret rested her chin in her hands.

It took several minutes for Margaret to shrug off her nagging concern with the mirror's image. Somewhat testily she resolved to avoid contact with that seeking, absorbing, judging object again, at least while in her present state of mind. At the table she showed the gilt-framed oval her back. Still, she knew it lurked there, just into the darkened hallway, holding the secret of her momentary accession to vanity.

An uncharacteristic Margaret muttered darkly, "And just keep your opinions to yourself, won't you, please?"

Breakfast was a brooding event. Memory of the mirror's reproach had not fully dissipated, and the hard, firm arms of her maple dining chair felt comforting and even necessary as Margaret gripped them for support that was not solely physical. A creature of conscious restraint, she would not have slumped down into the seat, but she was tempted. And much later, even after the somber-toned parlor clock had chimed ten, Margaret had not yet checked the cats' water bowl.

Rising from the table, she submitted at last to the day's demands. The cats would have to wait a while longer, as another delayed task took her away from them and in the other direction. Dispiritedly she trudged through the house to the front room, where she opened the heavy glass-paneled door and then the screen door.

Reaching toward the swaying wicker half-basket that served as a mailbox, Margaret made her first real contact with Monday. A quick rush of warm, scented air and a chorus of birds and summer insects greeted her, and she hurried to shut both doors that separated a too-bright front porch from the dark, cool entryway.

Her escape was not quite fleet enough. Sounds continued to pursue her even as she wrestled with wedging a heavy door over an uneven threshold and an immovable rug.

She was glad when the closed doors restored her separation from the outer brightness. The heavy wood muffled one final "Chirrrp!" as she left the morning concert.

Squeezing a bundle of mail in one hand, with the other she tested the long shade pull that was, as always, already drawn down. Brittle and imprinted with the etched glass panel's pattern from years of backing it, this long paper shade was never raised and thus never needed lowering. Only those infrequent visitors or salesmen who stood waiting for a response to the waist-level brass knocker ever truly could have studied the delicate design. Framed by the much-painted front door's top half, the fanciful pineapple decoration on the glass was a symbol of welcome and hospitality.

How contradictory, mused Margaret. Few indeed were the persons who crossed the threshold for social pleasure only.

Margaret then readjusted dusty lengths of ivory lace to restore the blocking of virtually all the morning sunlight. There was no need to shut the transom, for the one above this door, like the ones over several doorways in Margaret's old family home, was never opened. They all stayed closed, in bad weather and in good, and the rectangles of heavy glass in their dark walnut frames barely murmured even when violent wind slammed against the tightly shingled frame house.

In a less melancholy state of mind, Margaret would have relished the peacefulness that now settled over her household. Though scarcely cooler than the outside, the house was still a haven. Dead air and just-less-than-tepid temperature created a sense of suspended time. Nowhere was the impression stronger than in the parlor, just steps from the front threshold.

Barely discernable in the tightly draped room, the jewel tones of the antique upholstered furniture would surely by now have been faded by the white summer sun had that fierce morning intruder been allowed entrance. But Margaret was an efficient gatekeeper and all was as it had been for years in the elegant old room.

The worn yet dustless planks of the hallway whispered as she shuffled in hard-soled house slippers back toward the kitchen where her well-used letter opener awaited any bills in the mail.

There was that mirror again. Margaret resolutely stopped in front of the hall tree and stared at herself, and just as resolutely moved on without lingering or allowing for any more insolence from a piece of home furnishing.

Not that the mirror had always been so ignored or considered such an adversary. A repository for coats and hats of a bygone era, the slender six-foot upright rack had stood in the home's formal entryway but was moved by Margaret's father Stanley, at his wife's directive, to the much-traveled corridor by the kitchen. Florence had wanted it there for the family to use, she said, as a quick check on appearance; however, Stanley's fedora on Sunday and Florence's playful hats were quite possibly the only objects of dress that were ever checked in the beveled glass.

Stanley teased that it was a lady's version of a hall tree, shorter by a foot at least than most in other historic area homes. Delicate gold framing formed a graceful border that separated the mirror from the wood. Margaret's mother delighted not only in the mirror's utility but also in the carved acorns and leaves in the wood itself. These details she caressed as gently as she would have touched the face of a child.

"Flo, you don't fool me," her husband had joked. "You just don't want the sweet little thing to sit by itself in the front room." Florence had ignored him.

Indeed, here by the kitchen it became a part of the family. It gladly suffered galoshes puddling in its drip pan and downy winter coats lying on its chair-like base. The mirror changed colors with soft candles that Florence lit for no particular reason, and with festive Christmas lights that Stanley obediently strung in various directions and locations throughout the house.

On this day, the day of the mirror's rebellion, Margaret for some reason felt the sharp contrast between her mother and herself.

Mother had indeed known how to live with a flourish, and the house and grounds had reflected her love of life. Memories of lush, multicolored flower gardens she had nourished through hot Kentucky summers stood in stark contrast to the dead, unplanted area that Margaret could now see outside the dining room window. Where crystal filled with roses once brightened the table's center, a practical zip-lock bag containing stamps and a checkbook greeted Margaret as she sat down with the mail. The bag and the waiting opener were the only decorations now.

Empty cut-glass vases that gathered only dust in Margaret's house had, during her mother's reign, been stuffed with mismatched bouquets of riotous color, doused liberally with water, and moved at whim throughout an open, sunny house. Trailings and tiny wisps of stems and leaves and petals showed the path that the merry decorator had taken. Billowing white, starched organdy curtains sometimes threw the floral arrangements over, tossing them like children tumbling others at play. Florence had scooped up the brightness and had hummed as she simply placed it out of reach of the playful curtains, but never closed the window. Even when it rained, the windows stayed open.

Margaret put her glasses on, determined to waste no more of the day. Like it or not, there were things to be done. After discarding junk solicitations and paying a few small bills, she considered that at least she had tackled the mail. One task down. Following a cursory check of her perfectly dovetailed calendar of social obligations, she saw that there were no birthday cards or other personal mail that needed to be sent. The discovery left her inexplicably disappointed.

Moving mechanically and with an unfamiliar absentmindedness, she ran water into the half sinkful of dishes, emptied coffee grounds, and dumped the remnant of breakfast into the cat bowl. Even the small exertion left her perspiring.

Just three cats were on the warming back porch at this time of day, and the two half-grown kittens darted away at the rattle of the screen door. Only the mother cat fell quickly to eating the few morsels of bacon and egg, leaving crumbs and grease for her offspring to lick later.

As a general rule, Margaret had not named cats, for she professed no attachment to them. She did, however, notice that Dreamsicle was not around just then. They had become friends, after a fashion, the evening before. After attending church Sunday morning, she had not ventured out of the house until after the day had grown dark and cool, to scrape out supper's crumbs to the ravenous family of cats that convened by late dusk. Even on the Lord's day small creatures needed to be fed.

Margaret knew that the group lunge they performed was almost solely for food, but the pretty little orange-and-white female had stayed with her and arched her back for a caress even while the others descended wholesale upon the scraps. Margaret had given her a perfunctory stroke and meant to end at that, but found herself talking kitten-talk to this endearing wee one, to her own bemusement. Her mother had always been the one who was good with animals.

"Is it a sweetie? Is it a good kitty?" Margaret ventured.

Purring delightedly, the excited young cat applied remarkably sharp teeth and claws to Margaret's hand. Margaret withdrew from this untoward show of affection and hurried to retreat.

Dreamsicle, as she had been named by Margaret's niece, was not satisfied, and mewed her appeal for more attention even as the door closed. The small dream-colored shape lingered disappointedly on the wide top step.

"Why don't you go on, now? Shoo...Scat, I mean." Miss Denton was not skilled in pet language.

Although Margaret had finally slipped inside, two sharp, round, feline eyes remained fixed on the spot where the click had sounded. A guilty peep from above through thin gingham checks confirmed the tiny presence. At last, though, the kitten had given up and had scampered to the others. Margaret had firmly twisted the lock below the curtain and had gone to bed, duty fulfilled.

Now as Monday's midday sun produced a leafy pattern on the worn flagstone floor of the shaded porch, Margaret paused and wiped her perspiring brow with the back of her hand. She wondered briefly where the young cat might be, then quickly tried to reject this interest as too sentimental.

Although having consciously shaped and carefully burnished her resistance to involvement with other living creatures, she clearly felt a slight piercing of her armor. Had Dreamsicle's tiny kitten teeth and claws started it on Sunday evening? Margaret was more amused than she had expected to be by the connection she had drawn, and pleasantly aggravated at a certain unseen small creature.

"All right, all right. Dreamsicle, you should be satisfied. You've made me get all weak and silly. And you're not even around to get the blame."

Margaret looked around guiltily. When had she ever let her guard down so? The mirror had noted a different Margaret. She was, according to the judgmental oak object, not herself. Could a silvered piece of glass in a hewed block of wood have been right?

Flustered for some reason, she bestirred herself to put her thoughts back into proper place, and attempted to smooth the curly wisps of hair that had strayed from under the practical old gardener's hat. The house, although still only a few degrees cooler than its environs, would surely seem pleasant. Margaret's demeanor could perhaps achieve restoration there as well, as she would not be bothered by thoughts of small frisky animals.

But, being Margaret, she would complete her tasks before seeking her own comfort. In a brief sidestep, she removed her mother's floral apron from its hook on the one wainscoted wall of what the family had always called the inside porch, opening off the kitchen's southern side.

The room was so named from the days when it had held the cream separator and a table and chair for her father's hired man. It was, as now, only partially closed in. When Stanley Denton had bustled in and out, to Florence's pretended exasperation, the room had been a connection where the garden and the house flowed together.

Younger relatives on recent rare visits had declared the old cream separator and the three unpinged milk cans "quaint" and had left happily gifted with "antiques" that generous Cousin Margaret had been only too glad to get rid of. Margaret had divided the tools and had given the duplicates and extras to Edna Waverly for an Assembly of God yard sale. The two remaining double-grip cream cans of dented gray steel and an assortment of long-handled tools often wore dust that filtered in through the screened outer walls, but most of the fine particles that still wafted in rested only on a bare concrete floor.

Margaret swept the ancient surface today as she did every day about this time. Tasks were ordered in Margaret's household, and her day was full of accomplishment as a result. A few deft, broad strokes finished the job in the cleared room. Margaret rested the handle of her broom by the door to the kitchen, against the spot where old Frank Wilson had carefully settled one of Florence's bow-backed kitchen chairs to partake of his workingman's sustenance.

Without conscious effort, Margaret found herself reaching into empty space, as though to touch the graceful curve of a chair back, one coated with Stanley's good white paint.

Frank had clearly delighted in the noon repast that Mrs. Denton placed before him, with reminders that more was on the way. Florence had, in turn, reveled in his enjoyment.

"Mister Wilson, now you just help yourself to everything. I'm so covered up in vegetables this time of the summer, and Stanley keeeeps on bringing them in from the garden. Here, you let me fill up that bowl of Kentucky Wonders again. I absolutely believe they're the best bunch beans and they just grew in great big double handfuls this time..."

Florence's chatty accompaniment of superlative-laden commentary was as welcome as her food to Frank Wilson. This way he didn't have to talk but could simply continue to eat. The sight of a pretty lady in a bright flowered-y apron helped his enjoyment of the occasion, too.

And occasion it was, every single day that Stanley used Frank's services. This was no mere lunch; the Southern midday meal was always called "dinner," even in the humblest circumstances. Fried meat, vegetables flavored with the drippings, and cream or fruit pie were commonplace offerings. Frank's knobby hands gripped his iced tea glass for a second and third fill-up.

Time had very nearly erased all signs of those former days in that special room. Margaret could not remember what had become of the slight but stalwart white drop-leaf table that held Frank's dinnerware. Some of the colorful old dishes survived, she thought, but were in a locked cabinet somewhere in the pantry. Margaret left the bare room behind and entered her house.

The afternoon was quiet and uneventful. Margaret would have taken her usual nap, but something kept her awake. When the sun finally was setting, late on this confusing summer day, she walked slowly through the center hall into her kitchen and stood very still in the gathering dimness of the well-shuttered room. Curtains on closed windows plus old shade trees had made the room bearable through the hot summer afternoon. But the air was stale, and Margaret wanted to breathe deeply. She stretched her arms over her head and turned to face her judge again.

A stranger looked back at her from the hall mirror. Moisture had produced errant curls that she did not even feel like taming. Gone was all pretense of dignity. Her organization completely undone, she found herself wryly amused at the disheveled result and managed a crooked half grin. The hall tree remained silent, wisely wary of Margaret's shifting mood.

Margaret, checking her appearance? Margaret, pirouetting ever so gently, pulling her hair this way and that away from her face, flipping her curls with her hands and then shaking them loose in a frivolous halo framing a smiling face. Margaret? It must be an illusion.

The hall tree had its memories, though. Of them there was no doubt.

Appearance might always have been of limited consequence to Margaret, but it surely had not been so insignificant to her mother. Now the tree with its mirror had no fulfilling role, but when Florence lived, the mirror had a friend and had its opinions on a lady's appearance respected. After all, there was nearly always good news to tell.

The silver-haired lady had worn precisely applied and flattering makeup up to and past the day she died at a too-young age of sixty-four. Her strict instructions for replicating her careful daily beauty routine were left to be carried out in detail by Sharpton's only funeral home.

Margaret had not heard the conversation that had laid down the details, but she knew Flo.

"Good day, Miz Denton. How are you this fine day?" the spare, pale Howell Richards would undoubtedly have said. "How may I be of service to you?"

Funny word—"service"—just what she had in mind to discuss.

The smile would have flashed, the carefully kohled eyes would have sparkled even then, or especially then, as they always did when Florence was on a mission.

Did she really say—yes, she would have said, "Mister Richards, I do indeed have need of your—service."

Shy, reserved Howell Richards surely must have had his propriety tested. The third in a family of morticians, he had encountered his share of unusual requests but had managed to balance decedents' wishes with survivors' sensibilities. This, however, was no ordinary about-to-be-deceased customer. This was the former Florence Tapp, always a woman who got what she wanted, including avowed bachelor Stanley Denton. He had lasted to the ripe old age of twenty-eight before bowing to her applied three-weeks' charm. At least he had three weeks. Poor Mr. Richards had only a few minutes of pleasure in her presence before succumbing to her wishes.

Unlike the traditional floral tributes that the funeral home always supplied for other Sharpton funerals, there was at Florence's death a casket spray of what looked suspiciously like wild flowers, including day-lilies and even Queen Anne's lace, ("A weed, for lord's sake!") and vases filled to dripping with practically all the flowers in Florence's garden were on stands behind and around the bier. Friends and relatives wore quizzical looks when they heard, instead of the customary piped-in hymn music, the strains of Robert Goulet singing "Love Is a Many-Splendored Thing."

Howell Richards suffered the indignant stares and whispers, but remained loyal to his business arrangement and to the one who was more than a client. He shed a few tears himself, in private, of course, for the vibrant lady whose spirit he would indeed miss.

The lying-out gown—a luminous, slightly indecent rose chiffon that hinted at sheerness—and her makeup, just as luminous and slightly more indecent, provided the community with a buzz of talk that would have delighted the elder Denton woman. Perhaps the confusion she caused amused her even in death, judging from the caricature-like lipstick smile on the face in the casket. It gave an impression of one who was enjoying a last opportunity to shake up the staid status quo.

"Well, if that wasn't just plain vulgar!"

"You could see right through that thing!"

"You think they'll bury her with all those rings still on?"

"Dijou see those fangernails?"

…Was it possible for a corpse's smile to broaden?

Florence Denton had had the last laugh, or at least the last smile.

Today, three years later, the memory of sweet silliness caused Margaret to smile also. In fact, she laughed out loud and whirled to face the mirror in the hallway. She caught it pretending to nap.

In an ultimately unexpected movement, Margaret Denton bowed in gratitude, curtsied really, to her unprepared furniture. The small coat tree stood simpering in flustered disarray, bewildered by the turn of events. Things certainly were changing fast around here.

All at once Margaret seized the curtains, ripped them open, and attacked her kitchen.

The bewildered little rack watched in awe as its mistress opened windows and cupboards, retrieved some long unseen dishes from a red-trimmed white cabinet in the pantry, and set them out at odd spots on the countertops and utility surfaces. Locked away for years, the brightly colored, hefty vintage bowls seemed new again.

The tree recalled a Mr. Wilson who used to be served from them. He had been the one who had reverently hung his old straw hat on a brass hook, being careful not to scratch the beautiful wood. Returning the old man's respect, the tree had held its battered, sweat-ringed charge as gently as it would have carried the finest topper of a Victorian gentleman.

An alien sound filled the brightening kitchen. Unfamiliar as it was, its identity soon became clear: Margaret Denton was humming. Disconnected and of no particular individuality, the snatches of melody were old hymn strains. The corridor witness felt its wood glow in response.

The porch cats would profit from Margaret's cleaning frenzy. There were tidbits of meat from leftover meals, plus milk-soaked bread crusts and end pieces from bacon packages. In the friendly light from the window over the sink, the others fell upon the feast with enthusiasm, but from a special vantage spot on the step just below the screen door, Dreamsicle purred and admired the cook.

Colors and music and sweet promise swirled in its wooded memory as the exhausted hall tree nodded in luxurious tiredness. Its day had been full and rewarding, and one could rest when one's duty had been discharged faithfully and well. And it would be nice not to have to criticize Miss Margaret any more.

RACE TO THE RIVER

It was too much for Ben to believe.

Jordie said there would be gifts, not under the tree, but on it instead. Or maybe their lumps would show in homespun stockings hung to the side of the hearth to keep from setting them afire.

Probably there would be an apple, saved from harvest in a cool cellar along with potatoes and pumpkins. Jordie kept adding to the list of unbelievable delights, so that Ben dared to dream, too, of the smell of an orange—an exotic prize in Kentucky in 1914. Nuts were possible, some ridged English walnuts, pale and clean unlike the dark woods walnuts of the area, and small, smooth-shelled pecans.

Candy was likely, from the mother's own hand and her enormous black cast iron wood-burning stove, divinity and fudge and hard-ball drops made of syrup and hardened in the cold winter air. It would not be in the stockings, though, but in a bowl in the mother's aproned lap. From there it would be doled out by the piece to each child, from the oldest down.

Other presents were rare, but these alone would surely be riches to Ben, for he was not accustomed even to such simple gifts in his own home. It was not in his parents' house, however, that he would wake this Christmas, but in the Whistler home, where his grandmother was mother still. Here the children were his own mother's siblings, though just barely older or even younger than Ben himself, who was eight. His uncle-brothers, he considered them, had whispered to him the miracles of the Christmas morning that waited just beyond the night. Ben, however, had a hard time receiving such glorious prophecies.

"Jist you wait," advised Junie, the oldest. "Santy Claus will come, even, and he'll mebbe come by yer side of the bed and git yer own stockin' and put stuff in it."

Silent, heavy snow had covered the ground and the howling wind was blowing knee-high drifts long before Ben and the others—Jordan, the youngest, Ben's uncle but born seventeen days after Ben himself, plus Junie and Earl—had climbed the stairs. In a rush they had dived into the tall iron bed and fought with each other for the layers of homemade quilts.

Ben checked his socks just before climbing in and promised himself he would look for them again early as he could the next morning.

Waking in the pre-dawn stillness, he had forgotten about the socks but he knew something else he wanted to see. He breathed on a small square of glass in the left corner of the window. The only advantage to having been rooted over to the cold side of the bed by his three young uncles was being able to see out the window first, before the others woke. His pointing finger made carefully silent circles and the outside came into view through his secret opening.

What he saw by the brilliance of the crystal onyx sky, with a full moon shining its brightest, was a pure heaven of the whitest snow. Surely this was the whiteness of the robes the preacher talked about, that he assured his ill-clothed congregants they would all wear in the world to come. After a young life already lived in bareness and cold and emptiness of stomach and heart, Ben felt his soul burn with a summer's joy and he could hardly pull himself away from the shimmering view.

"Ben, git back in bed!" came a muffled complaint from the body nearest his. "You was keepin' me warm," fussed Jordie, the one who buddied with Ben as if the two were brothers.

Jordan, meanwhile, had gathered Ben's share of the scratchy woolen covers closer to his side, molding their shape to his.

Ben had no choice but to get back into the pile. With the uncurtained single-pane glass affording no real protection from the outside freeze, his bare feet and hands were fast becoming icy. He slid back into the bed and with main force pulled away for himself a portion of the black and brown patched cover-lids, Jordan giving way only when Ben had situated his back to Jordan's side and provided a bulwark again against the window's draft.

The top quilt was the kind his mother called a "comfort," and truly it was. The heavy string ties that bound it together tickled Ben's nose, but he kept his head as deep as he could in the warm mound of batting-filled covers. Faintly aware of pinfeather sticks from the feather bed, he nevertheless felt a deep contentment. Soon warmed again and lulled by the soft snores of the three Whistler boys, Ben slid into a sweet slumber until the late dawn of Christmas morning.

"You younguns awake in here?" Granpa Sam's voice preceded him as he swung open the chamfered wood door to the boys' upstairs room. His tall, lanky body and farmer's long legs carried him quickly where he wanted to go at an active near-fifty years of age, but the voice came ahead. Ben remembered thinking that Whiskey Sam, as he was called, always talked with a smile. It lit up his hollow, grooved cheeks and his Scots-blue eyes.

Things were different at home, with his own daddy. He started to push out all thoughts of home for now, but he missed Mother. Not seeing her when he woke up produced a twinge of loneliness, but he knew what was going on. His two older brothers Charles and Daniel, and his younger sister by four years, Lucinda Frances, were all farmed out to other kinfolks while their mother was giving birth to another baby.

As Lucy was only four, Ben did not think she would know what was happening, but he and Charlie and Dan were big boys and had seen cows and horses get fat and then lie down to have their young. Mother had been having to stand far back from the stove since the late fall, when the gleanings of the garden had called for a final canning even as frost was creeping closer. He did not want to think about her lying down and grunting like a cow, or especially a hog. For an awful second he had a vision of little Lucy Frances Hallum popping out from under their mother's long dress, the red-headed sister already big as now and fully done up in her one tiny smock and her curly hair caught in a bow, a fancy one such as she had never owned.

Such thoughts disturbed Ben's enjoyment of this morning, and he found himself not wanting to miss anything. He was glad to hear cheerful Whiskey Sam's voice and he sat up in bed with his uncles, wishing for a moment that he could do this every day. Of course, he would want to go on home and see his mother later, he swore with a guilty loyalty.

"I do believe I heard somethin' last night," Sam began, thoughtfully massaging his stubbled chin with a long, bony hand. His light blue eyes danced with some secret joy as he tried to sound serious, even somber. "It sounded like...well, it cain't have been...but it sounded like...like reindeer's hoofs a-pawin' up on the roof!"

Little Jordan disappeared under the covers again. The drama was too much for him. Ben was glad he was a growed-up boy and wasn't scared, he thought to himself. Besides, he would never let Sam Junior and Earl know if he happened to be. He held tightly to the comfort's edge.

Sam's laugh rolled all the way down the narrow plank stairs with him as he hastened to tell Lemery Jane about the little boys upstairs who were afraid of reindeer. Slapping his hands in glee, he declared loudly that he reckoned they didn't need any Christmas because they were such fraidy pants.

All four tousled-hair fraidy pants, still only in their long johns and unheeding of the cold wood floors, raced down the steps in their bare feet to claim the morning.

Four sets of eyes widened at the sight of the tree, trimmed by angels no doubt, with strands of delicate popcorn puffs and red berries from the Kentucky woods.

Slender hand-dipped candles in their pewter cups were lashed sturdily to hefty cedar limbs. A bucket of water stood near for dousing in case of a tipover.

True to the boys' predictions, Ben saw, Santy had indeed brought presents. Junie, Earl, and Jordie ran squealing toward the lowest branches where curiously distorted stockings were tied, drooping with their heaviness almost to the calico and gingham patchwork quilt on the floor beneath the tree. As he was only a guest, Ben stood back and did not give away any desire to get what was not his to receive. But Grandma Lemery motioned to him.

"Why, looky here, Benjamin, it looks like Santy Claus knew you would be here for Christmas instead of in your own home. He brought some presents for you, too," she said as she held up his own sock for him to see its lumps.

Ben instantly recognized his mended footwear and wondered at Santy being able to reach right down beside the bed and get one of each of his and his uncles' socks without waking them.

The glorious contents were too precious for him to consume right away, although he heard Junie—the name Sam Junior was called—crunching into his crisp red apple. Jordie and Earl were rolling their oranges to loosen the insides, and Granpa Sam readied his knife to make a small hole in the top of each child's orange so that the juice could be sucked out.

But Ben held his luxurious golden globe in both hands, reluctant to spoil its dimpled splendor. Seeing his hesitation, Lemery suggested, "Mebbe you want to wait on your orange, honey? I'll show you later how to peel it. That way you can have the juice and the flesh both."

Ben nodded, relieved at not having to relinquish his prize. He folded the sock gently around it, carefully enclosing the apple and nuts also.

In amazement he felt that the sock was not yet empty. He dug a hand, he hoped not too greedily, into its depths and came up with a tied package not half the size of the apple. Trying not to tremble, he undid the grass string and folded back the brown grocery paper. A carved horse, clearly the work of Granpa Sammy's hands, lay inside. The smoothed edges, the four stalwart legs, the head with eyes and mane, were all primitive and beautiful. Ben looked shyly at his mother's daddy and met his eyes, hoping he knew the happiness Ben felt, for he could not speak.

"Here, come and git the goodies," announced Sam. For some reason Granpa Sam had a gravelly, throat-needs-clearing sound to his usually clear voice. He was indicating bowls of popcorn balls made with molasses, and gingerbread man-shapes with frosting eyes and buttons. Cold milk brought from its winter cooling place in the lean-to shed was in a glass pitcher on the table beside the display, and four tin cups were there as well. Ben felt a great warmth at being included in the setting, just as if he were one of four Whistler boys. Though guilt about his mother threatened to surface briefly, he allowed himself to pretend this was his home, at least for now.

Grandmother Lemery busied herself with settling the four around the long pine trestle, two on a side, with her and Sam at the facing ends. She was glad to have little Benjamin Joseph Hallum at her table, with a name larger than his timid self, and could barely resist sweeping him into a comforting cuddle for his and her own sake. At forty-five she was the grandmother of four including him, no, perhaps five by now if Selena's baby had been born during the night. Selena and Lemera did not have much time together for talking of such things, but Lemera sensed that something was wrong in her daughter's home. Lucas Hallum was not the man that Samuel "Whiskey" Whistler was. Lemera drew herself up quickly, breathing a silent word of penitence at having judged another.

Hungry stomachs waited eagerly for the gingerbread and milk, but Sam had things to say first.

"Bow yer heads, boys, and give thanks to the Almighty for his grace and his gifts," Granpa Sam instructed, then followed his wholehearted pronouncement with a scripture and a ritual blessing plus words of gratitude from his own heart. Ben found the waiting unbearable but at the same time fascinating, for he had only heard such religious talk in a church building before. Of course, that would have only been the two times he had ever been to a meeting house, both of them when he was visiting earlier with the Whistler family.

"Whiskey" was but a nickname on the amusing surname, and it certainly did not apply to any alcohol consumed by this gentle man, as he drank none. The small Methodist church known as Jordan's Chapel, after Grandmother's family—the name reflected in young Jordie's christening—had in Sam and Lemera Whistler two servants as devout and humble as the Lord could surely desire. And with next to no worship experience, Benjamin understood no articles of faith, except that his heart felt peaceful when Sam and Lemery smiled at him.

Sticky hands and grubby faces, made worse by the unwashed scramble the boys had made straight down from bed to the early Christmas celebration, caused Lemery to shoo the group back upstairs soon after breakfast. They were charged with making themselves presentable in the small room where their one bed and a table with a white granite pitcher and pan for washing were the only furnishings. Slop jar and wash basin used, Ben imitating the others, the four boys achieved a degree of tidiness and showed themselves to her for inspection. Ben was surprised to notice the new mends in his britches—had Santy taken time to fix them too?

Grandmother Lemery was not too rigorous in her looking them over, Ben found with relief. She even laughed as she licked and spit to seal down their variously shaded straw-color hair. Grandmother's hands paused on Ben's head and patted it briefly before the spit sealing. The touch of her hands, scented with a mix of wood stove and gingerbread and lye soap, gave him an unexpected happiness.

"Papa," called Junie, who was eleven and becoming tall, "kin I help you with the critters?" His voice was tinged with alarm as he saw his father emerge through the room's side doorway from the lean-to shed, where he kept his work gloves and the milking pails. Sam was already in his outdoor coat and had wrapped his head and neck with two wool scarves that Lemery had knitted. Junie and Earl and even Jordan always accompanied their daddy outside in the mornings, and here they were all cleaned up like it was Sunday and everything was all done already. The day's early festivities had thrown them off schedule.

Papa replied strangely, "No, you boys just stay in for now and let me see about 'em. It's awful cold and they's a big snow out. Besides, you boys have got comp'ny to play with today."

Ben did not really want to be "company," but the others were getting out of cold morning work, after all. He saw them turn their looks at him, and felt special because they would surely be grateful to him. He was not prepared, however, for their hostile reaction.

Earl, the second of the trio and all of nine years old, spoke first, respectfully challenging his father. "But, Papa, we allus do the mornin' work with you. You cain't do it all yourself," he pleaded, frowning sideways at Ben for upsetting their familiar daily routine. Earl and his brothers would miss the dark inside of the barn, with the tender bick-bick-bick of the hens who roosted higher in the winter, and the sweet milk smell of the cow with her calf by her side. All three boys would hang on the door while Papa milked, changing out buckets as needed and offering to "spell" him if he needed them at the teats. And the sleepy old horse with her rough winter coat would endure their pats and rubs until they left her again to her standing doze.

Even Jordan, just turned eight, glared at Ben before speaking. "Us three allus goes with you, Papa." The statement turned into a whine that Jordie instantly regretted.

Whining was not allowed, even from the baby in the family, and the father was put out with all three of his sons for the resentment they were showing. Girls had been easier, he thought, but growed up too fast. The two girls were older than the boys by so many years, it was hard to remember how they were anyway. Sally, just twenty, was yet to be mother though wedded over a year.

But Selenie had her own babies now. Lord, five of them by now probably, and she was just twenty-four…and here was pore little Benjamin, never got to be the baby, and something wrong, something…

Samuel Whistler, always playful and fun, now edged his words with a righteous anger. "Don't you boys never be ugly to kinfolks ner strangers. It ain't Christian and I won't have it in my home," he warned quietly. "And this here boy that's come to visit, well, he is to be treated right and with a godly love. It ain't because he's yer kin, neither, but because he's here away from his home and his mama and daddy, and it's Christmas."

The three uncle-brothers had been sufficiently shamed by their father's soft words, and rushed to embrace him around the knees and waist in repentance. Jordan was first to turn his wet eyes on Ben and to reach out a hand to grab his nephew's fingers.

"I din't mean to be ugly, Benjie," he implored, "and I won't be no more." He looked up to his father for forgiveness and received a brisk head-rubbing that delightfully removed all of Lemery's spit-straightening. But the mother only laughed her comfortable laugh.

Ben felt her hands on his shoulders from behind and was glad to hear the laugh because it helped him not to cry. And under her laugh Lemera Whistler hurt for this child and for her own child, his mother, and for some unspoken sadness that both of them had to endure.

The boys settled into their holiday after all and included Ben in all their play-like games. His horse, and Earl's and Jordan's just like it, went in and out of Junie's gift, a tiny one-horse carved barn, all boys squealing with delight at their farm play. Each horse snorted many times and bucked and threw off its imaginary rider. Samuel Junior as the eldest had received a horse at an earlier Christmas, and now could be the expansive host, generously allowing his brothers and younger uncle to run their stock on his land and share his new barn.

Ben could detect no resentment any more. At first he thought he knew the source of their kindness to him, that they were surely afraid of their father's disapproval. As the morning progressed, however, he realized the sincerity of their own sweet spirits and marveled at the glow of love and forbearance in this home. But once again the thought of Ben's own home raised itself like a specter, and he felt a chill in the hearth-warmed room.

Something smelled wonderful. Grandmother Lemery's stove was only feet away from the fireplace and from the large poster bed. The rough-hewn table and chairs, shelves on the wall, and pegs for clothes completed the furnishings in this one downstairs room of the pine log house. Whatever the grandmother was cooking was wafting its way into Ben's nose and stomach with boldness, and its closeness was making it even more tempting. Lemery stepped deftly around the children as they played in the only clear space, between the bed and the stove, and also between the stove and the table, with the fireplace to the other side of a square.

Whiskey Sam came back in and shook himself off, dusting the boys with snow and lightly coating the coverlid on his and Lemery's bed, even sparking the fire in the fireplace and the hot pans on the black stove. The boys squealed with delight and pretend fear at the snow monster with his cold shower of white crystals.

"Ow! Ow! Papa! You're snowin' all over! Brrrr, that's cold!" Their various exaggerated complaints assailed their father, with loving hugs thrown around his wet-scarved neck and snow-caked pants legs.

But Lemery only laughed. Ben loved that sound, he decided.

Dinner was as good as the smells had promised. The largest pot yielded green pole beans, canned at the height of summer's bounty, now cooked to a fare-thee-well with fatback seasoning and dotted with small potatoes from the cellar. A cast iron spider pan from the hearth held a crisp cornbread pone, while other pans that took turns on the large stove's heat were carried to the table and put on thick pads to protect the wood.

Lids were lifted to oohs and aahs, as buttery mashed turnips, fat dumplings shiny with cornstarch and chicken broth, and hot peach cobbler sent up their savory steam. Thick slices of ham were lifted from the large skillet as the fat still sizzled and popped, and placed on a heavy china platter in the table's center. Lemery smiled with pride and Sam beamed up at her as she completed the tableau.

The boys prayed that the prayer of thanks would be short, but Granpa had a lot to say this day. The food was all still warm when they started to eat, but just barely.

The snow had hardened to a gleaming finish and the winter sun was shining its best in the gray blue December sky, rushing to complete its day. At 2:30 there would be only about two hours of daylight left, and the children had not yet been outside.

At Sam's beckoning, they made ready to go out and play. Junie, Earl, and Jordan pulled on their sturdy though well-worn outside clothes with their hand-me-down boots and gloves. Many had been the time that an especially playful day had necessitated repairs to the humble winter gear, but Lemera and occasionally Sam had cheerfully done the mending, joking with the children about their rough play.

Ben quietly pulled on his shabby coat and followed them outside. He stood to the rear of the others, trying to decide how to get out of the play he wanted so badly to be a part of. He had no shoes for the snow, only the one pair that had been patched many times and were not sturdy enough for much wetting and re-wetting. Sam and Lemery knew without his saying that he was afraid to ruin them more, for he would face some kind of retribution at home.

Lemery was fair to bursting. She wanted to cry out to Sam with anger at her son-in-law for the hurt she was seeing in her grandchild's eyes. Tears threatened to well up in her eyes and she excused herself to go back inside. Something surely needed a hard scrubbing, she decided.

Samuel Whistler was not usually at a loss for words, but this situation made a knot in his throat that threatened not to come out. He swallowed and coughed for thinking time and then made his decision.

"Every one of you all! Off with yer shoes!" he called vigorously.

Lemera knew she did not hear correctly. She went on about her work.

The four boys stood looking at Sam. Had he lost his mind?

"I said, off with yer shoes! You want to be pantywaists

all yer life? I want to see which one of ye will make a man the fastest!" he continued, not looking at any of the bewildered faces.

Long fingers gestured toward the river, nearly a quarter mile down a bumpy slope from the tall, thin cabin. The Cumberland shone in the late winter sun, a pink ribbon of glass beneath a black sawtooth line of trees on the other shore.

He fished in his pocket and brought out an object. The round flat disk gleamed as he raised it above his head.

"You see this here buffalo nickel?" he demanded.

A nickel! The four youngsters stood in amazement at the wonder of the fortune their father and grandfather held between two fingers of his left hand. What if it should fall into the snow or mud and somehow be lost?

With his right foot Whiskey Sam drew a line in the snow, horizontal to the run of the river below.

He issued the challenge. "Whoever kin run the course from here to the river, and get back first, gets the nickel!"

Astonished silence greeted his announcement.

After an uncomfortable pause, Junie, the eldest, managed, "But, Papa, what do you mean about takin' our shoes off?"

Ben was beginning to suspect a special dispensation for his lack of winter footwear, but there was nothing he could read in his grandfather's face, nor could he make eye contact with his elder.

"If'n you all wore yer shoes, some would be better'n others, some worse," Sam Whistler explained with a logic known only to himself. "If you're all bare-footed, you'll all have an equal chance," he finished, as if to say the situation should now be thoroughly clear.

Shoes and stockings began to peel off, in honoring obedience of the one who always told them the truth.

Even as he sloughed off his foot coverings, Sam Junior managed one last inquiry, "But, Papa, won't it make us sick? Mama says…"

Sam cut him off. "You sayin' you're goin' to be a mama's boy all yer life? If yer up to any speed a-tall, ye'll shake off the cold as ye go," he remarked calmly, without sarcasm.

However, he casually added, "But, now, boy, I reckin you're part right. These little fellers here have got lots other years to win a nickel…" and Sam Whistler looked intentionally at his own two younger sons.

Turning to Ben as though the thought only just then occurred, he declared, "So we'll make it a race between you, Benjamin, and my oldest boy for jist this year!"

Ben was stunned at being chosen for the pursuit of the fabulous prize, but held back his delight for fear of seeming forward. He also did not want to be put at odds with the others again.

As Ben stood speechless in confusion, Junie squared his shoulders to bear his family's responsibility, and said, "Yer right, Papa, and I will. I'll run first of my brothers."

Sam smiled at his eldest son and looked seriously at his grandson, "And, Ben, if'n you don't mind—if you would do me the favor—to be the other one in the race, why, I wouldn't git in as much trouble with Grandmother…" He jerked his head ever so slightly to indicate the busy, unobserving female figure in the house. He continued in a dropped voice only for Ben, "Them little ones might get the foot-ache or even the ague, and I'd never hear the end of it."

So Ben agreed graciously, nodding silently but with an overjoyed heart.

Un-shoeing completed, both boys stood at the line drawn by Whiskey's foot and leaned forward, waiting for the signal. They leaped at the sound of his voice, "GO!" and Lemera turned to look, almost dropping her mother's china platter.

Their course was simple. The sleek, hardened snow smoothed out the rough ridges of river's edge farmland and made for a fast surface, where the boys could have slid for fun instead, if they had not had a challenge to meet.

Ben did not know exactly why he ran so hard, except that the buffalo nickel was the first and only one he had ever seen that he could possibly have for himself. His churning feet, free of the poorly-fitting shoes, sped over the frozen landscape and he found himself out in front.

Sudden joy seized him as he realized he was already halfway to the river and in the lead. He wanted to whoop but instead turned on the speed even more.

Ben was breathing hard and the keen air in his face and mouth felt like the pin feathers in the Whistler boys' ticking. Stinging and darting, the air was as cold as the snow under his feet, but still felt good.

And in spite of the cold, he was glad to be able to run freely in his bare feet, as he did all the year except the coldest part.

It was then, Granpa would be shocked and angry to know, Ben sometimes did his father's tasks as the elder lay sleeping off the still's product. To keep from ruining the worn shoes when they were very wet, Selena's youngest boy worked in leather rags tied around his feet, with both cowhide and human skin having to be dried and restored afterward at the fire. The strips had to be kept ready for other errands at any time, including gathering more wood. Charlie and Dan had the father's old pair of boots they shared in spite of the separations between soles and uppers, and the holes that toes stuck out of, and would have shared with their younger brother Ben, but Daddy kept them busy working also. The two sometimes traded back and forth, each wearing one boot and a deerskin mocassin.

Ben's thoughts had carried him along over half of the frigid course's first lap. But now he saw Sam Junior gaining on him.

Junie's eleven-year-old legs were long and gangly like his father's, and he was closing on Ben in a lope. He grinned at his younger uncle with a victorious glee and caught up and passed him.

"I'm gonna have 'at nickel, Benjie!" he shouted into the wind as he lengthened his lead and dashed Ben's hopes.

Ben felt his heart hurt as he kept running, and he would have cried except that the river was nearing, and Junie would be turning soon, and would see Ben crying as he headed back.

Sam Junior was so confident in his winning run that he stopped at the river's edge and did a happy dance in the slushy ice, splashing the water high enough for Ben to see it.

For some reason Junie drew his foot sharply out and grabbed it, then seeing Ben approach the water's bank, quickly started up the half-frozen mud to continue winning the race.

Ben's feet were tough and hardened from wear, but he was afraid he had lost the race. Yet, somehow, he found himself gaining on his uncle on the way back. A little closer, yes, keep on, oh yes, he was drawing up beside Junie.

It was unbelievable. He was pulling ahead now, ahead of Junie. He could not understand it, but it was happening. He could even see the faces of the little uncles and his grandfather, now joined by Grandmother with her arms tightly crossed on her apron, as he closed to within half of the snowy field's distance.

But something was wrong. With Sam Junior. Ben quit running and slid to a stop, then turned to look back.

No longer running and barely walking, Junie was limping and every once in a while reaching down to grab his left foot. Was it a charley-horse or was the icy snow getting to his flesh? Ben wondered what to do, and then he did it.

Ben kept running.

Back to where Junie was.

He quickly reached him and got his arm around his waist and the two of them managed a slow-time finish to the race, stepping over the line in the snow at about the same time.

Grandmother already had towels ready for both of them, and proceeded to rub their feet briskly, even ordering Earl and Jordan to watch her and do the same. She did not talk to Granpa and did not seem to want to look at him.

A gasp escaped Lemera's stern-looking face. "Oh, no, Sammy, look! Your foot is bleeding! How did that happen?" she asked the boy, but turned to his father with a glare while waiting for the answer from her son.

"Um, I reckin I done it at th' river, Mother. I seen I wuz ahead and I done a dance and cut my foot on the ice at the edge. I knowed I done it, but I thought I could get back okay..." the boy confessed.

Mother applied more pressure to her foot rubbing and now produced a jar of amber-colored herb salve from within the deep pockets of her dress. She slapped it on without any further words and again showed the elder Samuel Whistler her back.

Whiskey Sam stood in thought, seemingly unaffected by his wife's anger. It took a while before he spoke, but as usual he measured his words. "I declare. What a race. And it wa'n't no win by one over th' other," he marveled.

Ben and Junie looked up together. Winning the nickel had been pushed out of both of their minds. But now it was back and Sam was saying no one had won it.

Sam continued, however. Rocking his gaze deliberately back and forth between the pair of runners, he then pronounced, "So I reckin I will have to decide. Junie..."

His hope crushed, Ben steeled himself to congratulate Junie. And it was right. After all, he had been injured and he would easily have won had he been able to continue.

But Granpa Sam was full of surprises. "...Junie, I know ye'll understand that Ben done the Christian thing, by stoppin' and pickin' you up and givin' up his own self for you. And so..."

Ben was open-mouthed and Junie was nodding in agreement with his father's wisdom. The son was becoming much like his father, Lemera noted in a restoring warmth for her two older Whistler men, foolhardy though they both were.

The cold, thick coin pressed into Ben's palm felt like a

chunk of the icy snow, but his fingers closed around it in a reflex and it started to warm immediately.

"Congratcheeations!" Junie called expansively, pulling loose from his mother's massage for a moment. "En I don' know if I coulda beat ye or not. You was real game," he announced.

The buffalo nickel spent its existence from then on, until Benjamin was sixteen and out working on his own, wrapped in a scrap of the same brown grocery paper that had held his first Christmas present. Selena—Mama—never asked how the visit went. With a deeper sadness on her face she nursed the tiny baby boy, this one named Elijah, and managed but one cursory head stroking for Benjamin, her third of the now five. But she did look wonderingly at her big eight-year-old as he went early to wrap up his feet by the fire and get wood in without being told. Something had warmed his countenance and his actions. There was no anger or resentment. He was simply different from the boy who had gone from home before Christmas. He even stirred the stew pot hanging over the hearth. And Lucinda Frances got a carved horse for the Christmas before her sixth birthday, when he had decided she could remember to keep it hidden away.

A MAN ON THE PLACE

"Why did you go away and leave me like that?" Susanna demanded of her husband.

Receiving no response, she continued, her clear voice rising with pent anger, "Didn't you care that I would be all alone?"

His dark eyes with only the tiniest pinpoints of light never blinked, never moved. Benson Digby was as flat and static as the paper he was printed on.

Susanna Digby, still Mrs. Benson Digby after nearly a year, sighed. There was really no use in talking to the stern black and white portrait of her dead spouse, she knew, but it helped to put words to her frustration.

She propped the gray easel frame with its 8 by 10 inhabitant back on the mantel, between a large conch shell from Gulf Shores, Alabama, and a dusty green candle in its tarnished brass holder. Dispassionately she flicked the carcass of an insect from the brass piece and watched the crusty creature join a quartet of fallen comrades on the floor.

There was one good thing about being alone, or at least with no husband, she admitted. Housekeeping was simpler. No one came into the house who cared, and she would not care if someone did.

She claimed a twofold right—"to be and to be let-be"— as Susanna had expressed it several times to convince whoever happened to be listening, usually only herself.

In the mirror above the mantel she saw a lie, a reflection of a moderately handsome woman living a full life. Her light brown hair's grey streaks had the likeness of intentional highlighting and made her look younger than she felt.

With the tips of her long fingers she caressed the pictures of their children, their baby-sweetness preserved in frames of colorful plastic and metal, and their brave graduation pictures in grown-up polished wood. All in their forties now and three of the four living far away, they were all but dead in her life too, like their father, Susanna brooded. The baby times, the eager childhood years, exasperating teenage moods, all the happy, everyday fun and noise were gone, and only emptiness echoed most of the time in her large country home.

"Mama! Mama!" An impatient masculine voice accompanied loud knocking and a metal-and-wood rattling at the back of the house. Her habit of hooking the screen door was aggravating to Selden, her son who lived with her. He was also the greatest challenge to his mother's being let-be.

"Whatchu want to hook it ever' time, Mama? Didn't you know I was comin' back inside?" Selden berated her as she padded across the black-and-white painted flooring of her pleasant kitchen toward him.

His flabby cheeks were red even though the summer morning and shaded porch were cool enough, and his nose mashed against the screen made his round face a flat, pinched plate. Did he know what a hanging-spider image he made, with his arms up and his palms high on the sides of the door facing? Susanna wondered.

Huffing his breath after the short trip from driveway to house, Selden whined, "What if you couldn't have got to the door? I would of been locked out!"

Susanna did not miss the implication that Selden would have been more concerned about not being able to get in easily than about finding his mother unable to reach the door, prevented by illness or injury or even death, heaven forbid. Why, she mused as she popped up the curved metal fastener that allowed Selden to fall in and rush to the kitchen, why, how could she be so inconsiderate as to die, maybe? It would just be very inconvenient to her dear, thoughtful son.

Selden had stopped scolding his mother, due to reaching the refrigerator. Having completed his tasks including checking the morning temperature and the weather in general for his mother, and the more difficult chore of checking out her car's tires per her gentle request, Selden was famished from not having eaten since breakfast, and it was half past ten!

He had found ham slices and deviled eggs left from the previous day's church dinner, and was filling a china plate with several of each, while studiously adding sweet pickles and Vidalia onion slices. Wearing her washed but permanently sauce-stained apron with a "BBQ Chef" pig on its front, Susanna stood with arms placidly crossing the porker's image and studied her son. He was currently deep in his element, in a level of satisfaction and accomplishment that rivaled no other. He was in the presence of and present with food.

Gradually becoming aware of his mother's stare, Selden managed to speak, but with his mouth full. "What?" he managed, although it sounded stuffed with ham and bread. "Whassa matter?" The words were accompanied by onion and pickle crunches.

There was no use in attempting conversation. Mrs. Digby just shook her head and reached into the Coldspot to get the milk. She poured a large glassful for Selden and he immediately lost even his limited concern for her state of mind. All was right with Selden's world—things were as they should be. His mother patted his sweaty, large upper arm as she passed out of the room. It was important that it was not the arm attached to the hand he was using to attack his food.

In the living room in front of the long-unused fireplace, she paused and sought Benson again. Her mouth opened to report her unfeeling son, but closed as quickly. This Kodak paper man would not be sympathetic about Selden's selfishness either, any more than he had been earlier about his widow's loneliness.

Susanna missed the urgency that came from having a worthy side-worker.

"Suzy?" Ben would say, "what say we go look at the chicken coop and figure out what color we might paint it?" or "Decide where you want that row of step-stones, honey. I got an idea how they might look mixed with flagstones and those reddish-brown pebbles from down on the creek."

Many of the projects never came to fruition, and several more evolved into unrecognizable versions of their first suggestions. The stepping stones eventually became a surround for a flower bed, and paint planned for the henhouse had been postponed in favor of keeping the building's primitive look and dragging ancient farm equipment to its sides to decorate it instead.

But something had always been going on. Something was planning, simmering, perking, bursting into the day's slowness to keep it alive. Now the tedium dragged it down and the weight was heavy.

Drained from a failing effort to keep her life seeming busy and fulfilling, Susanna was emptied, exhausted. Behind her clear hazel eyes a headache was beginning. She uncharacteristically collapsed into a plush living-room chair and did not even straighten the arms' crocheted doilies that one of the cats had pulled in strange directions.

Flicks was a long-haired alley/mansion cat who deigned to live, along with his sister Teas, in this house with Selden and Selden's mother. Now he lay in a shaft of filtered sunlight on an ottoman across the room. The mingled black and gray feline did not even offer his comfort to Susanna, and this was one time that she would have welcomed a warm, purring companion.

Susanna Jackson Digby, widow of Isaac Benson Digby, was sixty-seven years old, tall and strong of limb, blessed with good health and the amenities of home and comfort that many never attained.

And she had no life left. No one to plan with, start projects with, banter back and forth with about this boondoggle or another. No man on the place to hatch out grand schemes with.

Yes, there was Selden—ah, yes, Selden—and there

were the girls, all professionals, all married, and all active with their half-grown children that their grandmother got to see only once in a while.

But she knew that all of them, including Selden, loved her and would be upset to see her so depressed.

Well, maybe not Selden.

The slender, lank woman roused from her self-pity, rolled up the sleeves of her light blue man-style shirt and the cuffs of her gently faded jeans. Her clothes were beginning to be too loose for her now that she no longer enjoyed food and partook of it much as Selden did, sans cooking, refrigerator container to mouth, cleaning up leftovers. But hers was more a housekeeping motion than a savoring one.

She removed her pig apron and armed herself.

The vacuum cleaner and assorted cleaning tools were her weapons. She spent the rest of the late morning furiously cleaning the living room, removing insect corpses and cat hairs and green-machining the carpet.

Such cleaning activity had always helped her deal with worry in the past, when Benson was late from a fishing trip and she all but had him buried from drowning, when Sandy had stayed out past curfew with that too-good-looking boy she ended up marrying early, and when Susanna's own mother had been suffering a lingering final illness. There was something about pulling the house in around a person, clearing away any debris that threatened its unity, and centering one's family again, something that the sweeping, mopping, and shaking helped accomplish, if only in the shaker's mind.

The activity was refreshing and profitable, and it settled her a bit. But the mood was not entirely gone.

"Oh, Ben, I don't know how I'll make it, but I'll try," she murmured half out loud, but not to the photograph. She wanted so badly to say it to Benson that she just closed her eyes and repeated it. New was what she must be, what she must do. Some new thing surely awaited her, a thing that would make her life new again.

An early lunch was as she had become accustomed to it, taken this day in fact not even at the table but standing at the kitchen sink, peering out the window. Above the barn-scene café curtain panels and below the coordinating valance, the long vista that was the back of the Digby place opened itself before her. In the clearness between morning fog and evening haze, she could see down the rolling acreage even to the last barn, once used for the four old thoroughbred mares.

And it was thus, on this day with its depressing start, that a new thing indeed started to happen. What Susanna saw first was not accompanied by understanding. There were only small details, really, but she would look back later and see them as so obvious. She first began to think about the differences because the lawn was getting so hairy.

From the large yard outward through the far reaches of the place, behind the former chicken house and past Benson's burn-place that the Digby children—the girls, that is—demanded that she not use, a fringe was beginning to develop. The yard's grassy beard was growing mostly in areas farther from the house and especially around the three barns, as less and less mowing was being done these days.

Benson had always kept the property all trimmed, and bush-hogged the fields, up until the undiagnosed colon cancer made his belly cramp and he had to hang close to the toilet. Selden had grumbled but had hoisted his heavy frame onto the John Deere rider and had attempted to approximate his father's neatness on the roughly five acres that they called the yard. The results were uneven, but Benson was quickly past observing for the sake of criticism—as though he had ever been critical, or anything other than loving and patient, sweet and funny.

Susanna's eyes started with the burn of kept tears, and she grabbed a broom, flung open Selden's spider-lair door, and stepped onto the back porch. The thoughts that had come to her unbidden at the kitchen window scattered as she stood on the west-facing wood structure.

For an instant she could not remember exactly why she had come out here, but she soon realized it was somehow just to see the sweep of the place again, the long straightaway from the big white frame dwelling on its gentle rise, down through the bowling-green fairway that only leveled out and then rose again at the barns. But it was getting away, this and that not repaired, the edges of the yard closing in more each week, weeds taking over the fence rows.

Rangy bushes and odd, skinny trees were establishing themselves in the downhill garden areas where Benson had happily tended his special, extra "crops." Zinnias, marigolds, hollyhocks, and bee balm were his simple delights, but he might dabble as well with yellow tomatoes or a funny kind of Chinese cabbage out there in the nether reaches of the downward-sloping yard. Susanna could see him dabbling out in his "workshop," she kidded him by calling his peculiar little garden. First one or the other would raise a hand in recognition; then they both would begin to wave vigorously, like childish sweethearts, when she was on the porch and he was in his happy green laboratory.

Now she strode with a kind of vengeance across the grey painted planks and attacked the nearest object, which happened to be a small throw rug at the top of the steps.

Grief and anger, still unresolved—would they always be?—swept over Susanna, alone on the pine-planked deck that needed water-sealing again and would not get it, by Benson or probably anyone else.

The throw rug had given up. Beaten into confused submission by her angry and unconscious thrashing, its fibers were stressed and some were flying loose and scattering down the wide steps to escape.

Susanna realized that her sweeping had been unnecessarily violent, and shuddered at her loss of control. She started to pick up the mistreated mat to take it inside, but hesitated, to take one last, lingering look Staring down the long, lonely view—the one so empty now—she saw it.

The outhouse.

That it had always been there went without saying. That it had been unused for years, no, generations now, also needed no saying. But that the tall grass in front of its weathered gray oak door was pushed down for ease of entrance after decades of non-use—that was worth saying!

"Who in the world…has someone been using that old privy?" she asked half aloud, her words sounding small in the wide open outdoors. "Why," she answered herself, "I believe someone has, all right."

Her blue-handled straw broom having fallen to the porch with a slight bang, Susanna cupped both hands like a horse's blinkers to block the sun that was now nearly overhead but still behind her.

Yes, she was right. Even from her distance, because Selden had been less and less meticulous about the mowing, she could see the long grass in front of the old necessary-building. There was no necessity now for its use, however. But the tall blades were definitely flattened in front of it.

"Ah, that's funny!" Susanna laughed to herself with more than a little relief. "Billy and Evan had never seen an outhouse. Probably Selden just had to show them."

Turning to re-enter her house and to shut the back of the house away from the early afternoon sun that would only get warmer and warmer, Susanna was satisfied with her own explanation.

She even chuckled again, thinking of the whole gamut of bathroom humor that young boys, especially the age of her nine- and eleven-year-old grandsons Billy and Evan, found so irresistible. When they last visited, Selden must have "enlightened" them on the use of the ancient building, complete with information about catalog pages, snakes, bees, and all the various elements of the outhouse experience in the lives of farm children everywhere.

Selden was in the darkened living room with only the light of the television set on. Showing was a TV Land re-run of "The Andy Griffith Show," which her forty-two-year-old son counted among his favorites, but she doubted he was really watching. She saw his profile against the color screen's brightness, and it appeared that the late or repeat breakfast with the ham and its accompaniments had truly been comfort foods. A low whistling snore reached her ears.

Susanna felt better. The poor porch rug had absorbed a lot of her emotion, she guessed. And Selden, aggravating as he was, was at least here in this husband-emptied house with her. It was good to have a man on the place, even if it was Selden.

As she puttered in the shade-darkened rooms, dusting, picking up, gathering a small laundry load, Susanna gradually realized a degree of contentment with her day after all. Despite her challenge to the starkly inanimate photograph of a departed husband, with her loneliness crying out in anger and frustration, she had been gifted later with the memory of her smiling, animated lover in the outdoor place that was so special to him.

And his mother even had a warming thought for her only son, with the conclusion she had reached about the outhouse having been disturbed. Selden's explanations of the outhouse's use and adventures for his curious nephews would have accounted for the appearance that someone had recently opened the door to the antique structure.

Susanna's hands dropped the plastic clothes basket, spilling the meager load of unmentionables.

It did not make sense after all.

There was no way Selden could remember the outhouse being used. "He's only forty-two," she reminded herself. "Even when Tammy was a baby, we had running water!"

Generations and experiences overlap in a person's

memory, Susanna knew, and it bothered her to admit that she could confuse the ages of family members, especially her own children. The baby in the kitchen washtub, with kettles of warmed well water from the wood stove, would have been Betty, not Gail or Tammy, her third, and definitely not Selden. He would never have experienced the old ways and might never have, in his infinite lack of curiosity, even wondered what the outhouse was used for.

Who, then, had opened the door?

Susanna had a new worry. She supposed that she had taken for granted that the door was tightly shut, for fear that a child or at the very least a small animal might have wandered in and fallen through the old two-hole bench. With grandchildren visiting on the place now at random times, the idea frightened her. She would have to check, she promised herself. As she prepared for bed, she set the idea firmly in her mind and would wake up remembering it.

Before Susanna roused the next morning, Selden had sneaked down to the kitchen and, according to the evidence, had fed himself a large combination breakfast, including Pop-Tarts, cereal, doughnuts, jelly, and milk. Nothing was cooked; Selden did not cook. He had already left the mess and escaped to his room. No chores to be caught having to do this morning, his moves implied.

His mother realized he had outdone himself the day before when he had checked her tires for her. He had to be desperate this morning to escape her plans for him—and she had none, really—if he was willing to watch the early showing of "Bonanza" on a 13-inch black and white set that was somewhere among the mess on his dresser. Susanna could hear the familiar, sweeping musical theme and then the funny, high-pitched laugh of Little Joe. Selden would be occupied for a while and was hiding out from his mother anyway. This actually suited her plans quite well.

She welcomed the early morning peace, except for the mess on the table, counter, and floor. Her own breakfast consisted of juice and toast with a bit of apple butter and two cups of coffee. She would need the caffeine, for she had a task to undertake. And no time like the present.

Susanna pulled on her light gray galoshes that held a pair of red slip-on flats. The yard would be wet, but at least the mowing was a few days old.

It felt risky, to be walking down the yard, so far from the house, and knowing that no one was watching from the house. She could be anywhere, lost or confused, disoriented like those senior folks she felt herself joining, some of whom were found when a pond was drained or a hiker screamed at the sight of human bones in tattered bits of clothing.

But Susanna stepped quickly and surely, as her feet walked away the months that she had avoided this place deep in the yard. Dread was replaced by a sense of adventure. As she neared Ben's old mystery garden, the subject of so much of her affectionate teasing, a lightness of heart prevailed in synch with her light, sure steps on the rolling ground.

All but carried away with the memory that was revived by being in Benson's old arena, she nearly forgot what she had come for.

Yet there it was, now just about twenty feet on down

past the disappearing garden spot. The rough, grayed outhouse, like a lady past her prime – when was that point, wondered Susanna—was rougher up close, lined deeply and softly crumbling while maintaining a dignity in the midst of ruin.

And it had been opened, not just once but often and lately.

Susanna breathed her lungs full of the fresh morning air, sensing she might need it, walked straight to the privy and pulled at the half-rotten wood door. It opened easily.

Her eyes adjusting slowly to the darkness, she saw little at first, then only the expected shapes in the darkness. The venerable two-hole plank, swaying a bit and curved up at one end, was still there. So were dangling remnants of cobwebs and shriveled leaves and debris and—she caught the slightest whiff but it was unmistakable—the faint scent of human use.

Horrified, she backed away quickly and whirled around, hoping she was not really looking for anyone, but wondering who would have felt it necessary to use this vermin-ridden outpost when even the woods would have been more hospitable in an emergency. She could not fathom why anyone would have used it more than once, for sure. And any thoughts of Selden or her grandsons succumbing to curiosity to this extent went completely away.

Her plan had been to use this downward trek to the building to do some subsequent walking down memory lane as well, specifically to check out Ben's old playground. She had hoped perhaps to find a stray Chinese cabbage or a surprising ground cover of bee balm. But the ground was hard and stubbly and barely resembled a garden place any more. Some of the deepest furrows had become jagged gullies. And the apparent habitation of the old outhouse had left her disconcerted.

She would come back, but with a weapon.

Early the next day, during Selden's and Marshall Matt Dillon's morning communion deep in her son's locked room, and before she had time to back out, she made herself enter the small chamber that Benson had called his "sports room." The description was mostly a joke, as it was only a locked storage area for his gear, in what had been a primitive lean-to shed off the far end of the kitchen. Barely over six by four feet, it had existed from the house's former days as a cabin.

The Digbys themselves, having come into the rural western Kentucky region as "outlanders," all the way from southern Illinois, had never known anything of its original use or inhabitants. They figured that it might have served as a haven for a cow and calf in a harsh snow storm, perhaps, or for a pioneer woman's store of canned and "rolled" storage—pumpkins, gourds, and so on, trundled into a cold room that would preserve them through most of a Kentucky winter.

Now Ben's scarred wood puttering desk, just a table top a yard wide on each side topping four recycled legs, nearly filled one end of the room. It was still laden with his odd collection of nature's trash and treasures, which in their soft coat of fine dust shone a bit when Susanna's kitchen light hit them. The dangling bulb in the upper darkness came to life when she pulled the string. Ben's treasure pile became a shabby clutter. It seemed unfair that the bulb still lived, and her husband did not.

The smells in the room from its distant past use were faint but recognizable. This room had Benson's scents in it, and his wife almost could not bear the way they assaulted her senses and her memory. Old hunting clothes and an assortment of trappings of the sportsman's life that he had loved still had their solid, meat-providing, manly smells.

She could remember burying her nose in his wood-gathering jacket just after he died. The tears had come strongest then, as she wept and wailed for the strong body and stronger heart that had once filled the rough fabric.

His best sporting goods like the Belgian Browning gun and boxes of shells that Ben had kept stacked neatly had been given to the sons-in-law or saved for eleven-year-old Evan, but Susanna knew what she was looking for in the windowless room.

Betty, the mother of Evan and his younger brother, would have exploded if she had known it was still there. The boys were curious and the danger was real, of course. A handgun was deceptive, maybe looking like a toy. But Susanna had a secret.

Turning Benson's "chair" on its side, she flipped a none-too-obvious tab of her handy husband's creation, and the base of the furniture, nothing but a heavy nail keg, separated from a round wooden box that had been the seat itself. Then she pried the box open, and there was the pistol, along with its matching ammunition.

The .38 special, its blue-gray body glinting in the eerie orange glare of the bulb above Susanna's head, felt cold in her hand. She laid it on the rag rug montage that covered the rough board floor and spun the empty chamber open. Hands trembling, she loaded six brass bullets in the slots and closed the chamber with a roll and a snap. The metal click was not loud, but she jumped. She even listened briefly as she thought she heard a sound in the house, maybe a step, maybe Selden?

She pushed away the thought, knowing that her nerves were suffering from handling such a deadly weapon. And now it was truly deadly, being a double-action weapon, for it would need no cocking, no preliminary backward pull, and had the potential to blast its tearing load into a human target with the right amount of exerted pressure.

Susanna brushed her jeans after the tiny room was closed away again. The dust and cobwebs wanted to cling to the hard denim seams, but she managed to get most of the material clean. There was more effort expended in washing her hands, slowly and under very warm water with a bar of tough workman's soap that she had found in Ben's things. The water was hot and steaming before she felt cleansed, though. The memories from the room and her lingering unease over what she might have discovered in the deep part of the yard were harder to remove.

Placing the gun on the worktable that was hers only, beside the no-Selden land of her kitchen stove, Susanna carefully covered it with a stack of laundered dish towels.

The entire capacity of her four-cup coffee maker would certainly be pressed into service today.

It was nearly noon and Sheriff Andy time before she slipped out of the kitchen and closed the back door behind her with a soft click. She had left Selden a large display of food on the antique porcelain-topped table in front of the refrigerator. A plate of cornbread, the crockpot full of beans and ham, and a still-warm apple cobbler were bait to catch Selden, to keep him from approaching the windows where he could observe her through the curtains. Maybe he would scarf it all up or abscond to his room with it as stolen goods while she was outside. She didn't want him suddenly to develop a never-before tendency toward curiosity now in his early middle age, just when she didn't need him to be looking at what she was doing.

Retrieved from the back of the hall closet, her long-bodied plaid blazer with its unfashionable padded shoulders and wide lapels had handy large pockets, and the right one was weighted down with the unnatural heft of the loaded gun. Odd-looking for a summer day, the jacket would have attracted attention if anyone had been observing, Susanna knew. However, as she had realized earlier, it was also a peculiar feeling to think that no one would be watching, for although she wanted to do this alone, the loneliness of her mission was frightening too.

Her trek to the outhouse this time was direct and quick. Pausing only slightly, she skirted around to the right so she could check for anyone inside without getting too close. The door was still ajar from her earlier visit and in fact the angle of the door opening appeared not to have changed.

Susanna's destination was the trio of once-active barns. Beginning with the nearest one, she would search all three if necessary. She proceeded exactly as she had planned, a farm woman used to dealing with invasive creatures in her stock and her crops. This trespasser might be different, she granted, but she was so far making her approach the same—quiet and direct and stealthy, with no waste of movement.

And as a result she discovered him.

With one hand firm on the unbarred door of the second building, she pulled it outward and pivoted herself inward in a fluid movement, and with the other hand lifted the gun and held it confidently, loaded and pointed straight at the man in the barn.

He was a young man, looking not much more than a boy to her sixty-plus-year-old eyes, slight and bony and terrified of the gleaming weapon in her grip.

His hands flew up in a gesture of surrender even before he scrambled to his feet in the shadowy interior of the stock barn. Susanna was startled by his quick move and thrust the gun forward, scaring him even more.

"Please, ma'am, please!" he begged. "Please, I ain't got hardly any money. But you can have what I got."

Susanna was hearing his words and taken aback by them. It seemed that she was the trespasser, not he, in his view.

"Whose barn do you think you're in, boy?" the armed woman demanded. "Did you think I wouldn't find you? Who are you and what are you doing here anyway?"

The young man seemed to be trying to find a question he could answer without angering the stern, dressed-up woman with that awful gun in her hand. And it looked like she meant business and could use the thing, or else just not keep it from going off.

"I'm, I'm Brian David Kelley," he managed but kept his hands up. "I just thought it might be okay."

"I didn't steal nothin,' " he hurried to inform the

woman, for he had just realized that she might think he was a thief. "I had a baloney sandwich with me and I drunk some water out of the cattle trough…"

Susanna's hand was hurting. The necessary tension to hold up the leaden pistol was making the tendons in her wrist and arm begin to strain, and the hand threatened to shake. She decided to lower the gun slowly and steadily rather than let young Mr. Kelley think she was shaking with fear.

Her target now managed to breathe, although he kept his hands up, taking no chances.

"You haven't told me why, though," Susanna commented tightly, "why you're on my property, using that old privy and hiding in…"

Brian heard the old-fashioned word and at first did not understand it, but a subtle gesture on the lady's part in the general direction of the outhouse cleared it up. He was embarrassed that she must have sniffed him out.

"I just didn't have no other place for a while," he explained, "and I thought it was better to use the old outhouse than to mess up your barn…" He faltered, dreading for her to start imagining what a trespass that would have been.

Susanna held the gun by her side but grasped it tightly all the same. She seemed to Brian to be thinking over what he had meant as a gesture of considerateness. It could indeed be interpreted as a lesser evil, not soiling her barn floor.

She kept her unconvinced stare right on him, though, the look that a parent or grandparent keeps to maintain the distance of authority and of generations until a settlement of differences is reached.

She said evenly but with emphasis, "Now, young man, you have still not told me why you needed to be here, in this place of all places, to do your business in any part of it. You had better answer me before I decide that I need to have you run in."

With that proclamation, Susanna lowered her left hand into a jacket pocket and pulled out yet another weapon.

She flipped the cell phone open and it responded with a beep that showed its readiness to assist in running him in, if needed.

Brian believed her readiness and wanted to avoid an arrest. He was starting to think of ways he could just take off, run out of the barn and toward some hiding place. He did not, however, know the area that well.

Looking down at his grubby jeans and the tennis shoes with long, dirty strings, Brian decided to tell her.

"I ain't proud of it, but I run away. I just couldn't stay. My mama had left and took Shellie, she's my little sister, and I stayed to try to keep working around with the neighbors for a few dollars here and there. But he started hitting me more and more and I run up and butted him hard in the belly and he fell down and was all out of breath but glaring at me. I knowed I couldn't be there when he got up. He woulda maybe killed me..." The long speech left him breathless and he stood waiting for her response.

His listener was stunned. This man – boy – was how old? She had revised her original estimate of early twenties downward to where she was now convinced that he was more likely in his middle to late teens. She ordinarily tried to rank youths according to the current grades in school of her brother's local grandchildren. However, she sensed that school was perhaps not a correct measure of this one's maturity. He might not still be attending school at all, and his education thus far appeared to have been a less than civilized one.

Her right hand went to her head in a gesture of frustration, and Brian ducked wildly, seeing the large gun wave upward and dangerously. He now held his arms out at his sides and appeared to be on the verge of butting another person in the belly, this time the only other person in the barn with him.

Susanna saw the hurt and fear in his eyes, and rushed to apologize. "Oh, no, I'm so sorry, I wasn't waving it at you...I was just...Oh, anyway, I'm sorry I scared you. Here, I'll put it away."

She gingerly pocketed the weapon. Brian did not relax much, but maintained his defensive posture.

Mrs. Digby pleaded, "Let me help you, Brian. You're just a kid, I see now, but I have to do something. Your mother will want to find you; this man—your dad, your step-dad?—may want you to come back and he might be different..."

This mother and grandmother who was all for protecting children from abuse could not believe she had just said that.

Brian still stood watchfully, poised like a bird ready for take-off. He disregarded her words, as he believed no one, no soft talkers or harsh ones either, all liars and ready to hurt you.

In the silence that followed, Brian had nothing left to say, but Susanna's mind worked at processing what she had found.

Brian's brave young face had hardened, yet weakness was betrayed in his quivering chin. Susanna had time to observe his wasted appearance. What she saw was not ravaging by drugs or dissolute living, but a sad child's near starvation. The child and the situation cried out for feeding.

Selden did not ask at first. He searched around a bit, even peeking under folded dish towels only to find trays of clean utensils and extra paper napkins. Grudgingly, he spoke at last.

"Mama? What happened to the rest of the cornbread and them beans and ham that was in the crock-pot? I can't find them and I figured there was some left," he pouted.

Selden was wishing he had gone ahead and gotten all the food and taken it to his room, but at the time Mama had been out of the house, gone to town or something, and he figured he had all afternoon to wander back to the kitchen and load up another plate or two, long before supper. But here it was just barely half after two and all the rest of the food had disappeared.

"Mama?" Selden wondered whether Mama was getting where she couldn't hear, or maybe going to be like those people who just suddenly forgot how to do everyday things. "Mama, you hear me? I can't even find it in the fridge," he prodded. Maybe she had put it in a dresser drawer or something. He heard of an old woman in town who did things like that.

Selden's mother turned, smiling, to her hungry son and said the oddest thing. "Well, honey, you'll just have to make do with what you had already. There was someone else that needed the rest of dinner worse than you," she said matter-of-factly as she ran hot water over the someone's dishes in the sink.

Selden stood amazed as Mama continued, "and I have hired some help so you won't have to worry about putting yourself out so much working for me..."

Even Selden knew the reference to his working was exaggerated.

"His name is Brian and he will be living in your daddy's old office in the horse barn—you know, the tack room Daddy fixed up when he had to spend so much time with the foals and mares. It has electric and water, though it will need better than that old cot, plus a few housekeeping items to make it more homey," she chattered on in a calm, happy manner that dumfounded her son. "I told him you would get the truck and take him the sofa bed that used to be in the den. I'll run sheets and so forth down there later," she added.

Selden was left standing in the kitchen with a fork in his hand as his mother wrung the dish cloth and carried it out to dry on the porch railing. She was humming.

Susanna would tell Benson Digby tonight that they had added to their family again, though this time a full-grown boy. Or just enough lacking being full grown to enjoy finishing him up proper. This wasn't like the four times she announced her "condition" to her husband when their natural-born children were going to join the family. Just the same, she would surely see Benson's eyes sparkle at their newest project, even if they were on that Kodak paper.

SOMETHING GOOD

"I bet she died with her tags on," was the way I heard it whispered. It didn't make sense at first to me, until I saw the proof for myself. And you can put that in your magazine story.

It was probably either the nicest thing or the worst that a person could have said about Miss Gwendolyn, like either she was a smart shopper in no hurry to wear the bargains she bought, or a spendthrift, lazy person who just bought and bought and piled it back. I didn't render any judgment as to which way I felt, and Gwendolyn Mattingly didn't let on as to how she took it—she was dead, after all.

When Mayjo and I went through the elderly woman's things, we started noticing right away what people were talking about. There were these price cards and string tags all still attached to her clothes, either tied, stapled, or sewed on. The clothes were from long-gone local dry goods stores and from big stores like Penney's and the Federated Store. My kids and grandkids don't remember a thing about that kind of store being here at all in Luten,

Kentucky. All they know is the Wal-Mart and Mickey D's and stuff. When I was growing up here in the 50's, make that a little into the 60's, why, you had a lot of small places to shop.

But Miss Gwen's things were that old and older, back to stores I never even heard of myself. Did you know that receipts used to have like "192__" already printed on them where you could just fill in the year in the nineteen-twenties? I personally didn't know it, but then again these were the first sales slips that I ever saw from that far back.

Pretty things Miss Mattingly hadn't ever worn were still lying inside their cardboard boxes, wrapped in delicate tissue paper and folded just the way a store clerk would have done them. The carbon-copied receipts, all yellowed like the tissue paper and the boxes, were there, too, just inside the top folds of the paper. Even though I could still read the faded blue handwriting on the red lines, I couldn't believe what little some of those fine things cost!

Besides all the new skirts and shirtwaists and even suits and dresses with the tags attached, there were Gwen's regular clothes. These were the ones that if you ever saw her, she was wearing, and what I would have sworn were all she owned. Do I ever know different now!

But that's the way things were all through the house. I mean, there were her wearing clothes and then there were her put-up-and-never-touched clothes. Between her two different wardrobes, I started calling them, they had all of her closets full and running over. Just one example—elegant felt, straw, and sequined hats with cardboard shapes circling the insides were stacked in tall, labeled hatboxes in the upstairs hall closet of that enormous, run-down house, but dozens of others, their feathers gone astray and scattered all over, would be dumped willy-nilly in the bottom of the same closet.

Satin lingerie and long, shapely slips and never-worn bras in different shades of creamy colors, with teeny little silk straps still gathered up and fastened with metal clips, were on hangers (hangers for petticoats and brassieres, mind you), I guess some long-gone way of making sure that no straps showed—ever. But piles of holey underwear and yellowed, wrinkled unmentionables were stashed, a disgraceful mess, in the bottom drawer of a heavy old mahogany bureau in the front sitting room where Miss Gwen had died.

When Mayjo was in the room she got all nervous, but not me. It used to bother me to be where somebody had passed away, but I've pretty well gotten over it.

Back about three years ago I just accidentally found myself in a room with the corpse of a Mrs. Weeder, when Mayjo and I were called in to do that cleaning, too. Mayjo had backed out on the job and I didn't know why. Come to find out the dear lady was laid out right there in the parlor. The ceiling light was so dim, I had almost backed into the coffin while I was running the sweeper. It scared me and I might have screamed, but there wasn't supposed to be anybody alive or dead in the house besides me and Mrs. Weeder that I knew of, and I didn't want to find out that there was.

Then—after I turned a few lamps on—I decided it was funny, so with nobody else around, I just had myself a grand old time talking really quiet to Mrs. W. We discussed ladies' matters, me complimenting her fine house because I was, after all, the visitor.

"Yes, ma'am, I do believe this is the finest parlor, but if it was mine, I would air it out more. What's that you say? You like it dark—easy on the eyes that way?"

Maybe she was about the most charming person I ever worked for. She didn't complain about how I did or didn't clean, never said a word, and I think I worked extra hard to clean her room up just so, since she would be receiving company the next day. When it came time to leave, I kind of hated to think of leaving her there all by herself for the time being, though. It's not really decent for kinfolk to leave a body alone—unless it's in a funeral parlor, I guess—without some of the family sitting up with it, but none of her bunch had got there yet. After I had put my coat on and turned the last light off, I felt for the doorknob in the dark.

"Nuhweemah!!"

I just about jumped out of my skin.

It took a minute to realize I wasn't with Mrs. Weeder's body at all—that was only in my remembering—but here in Miss Mattingly's house, and the scary sound was nothing but Mayjo calling my name, Laveda.

Mayjo's head was deep in that upstairs closet of hats, so her voice sounded muffled. I thought her stuffed-up hollering was funny, but when she heard me laughing, she was mad at me.

"Laveda! You about to take your turn at this?" she demanded, puffing upwards from one side of her mouth to try to dislodge a feather from her hair. " 'Cause I'm tired of doin' it all. I never seen so many CLOTHES!"

I thought that she looked silly with Gwendolyn's hat feathers in her hair, like a many-colored bird that was either molting or couldn't figure out what color to be. But

I figured maybe I better not laugh at Mayjo any more. She had helped me get cleaning jobs and she was a really good, hard worker to work with. Of course, I was braver than she was.

Well, anyway, we cleaned top to bottom on that house, and we needed a whole room just to set out and pile up those confounded clothes of Miss Gwen's. Once they were out of the way and in one place for the family to decide what to do with them, it was easier then to scrub, launder, polish, and otherwise get the house all spick-and-span for when the maiden lady's nieces and nephews would show up.

We picked the parlor for the boxes. Too bad Miss Gwen wasn't laid out there, or I could have talked to her like I did Mrs. W., and I would have given her an earful about that mess of clothes. She had been dead and buried a week or two before we got the job on her house, though.

"Miss Gwen," I would have started, "I'm Laveda Stiller. You don't know me, but my momma was one of the nurse aides out at the hospital, and she nursed your momma a while back when I was a youngun. Momma did that special duty nursing on the side and I believe she came over here to your house. 'Course, I don't remember any of it. But I guess you might, since you were already old...er, growed up."

Well, that wouldn't exactly have made a hit if I talked like that. Since she was dead anyway, I didn't fool any more with thinking how I would explain myself. But I would have liked to say, "You sure made a lot of work on Mayjo and me, with all that muddle in your belongings. What in the world did you mean by saving all these..."

Mayjo interrupted my pretend speech to Miss Gwen.

She wanted me to help with some more of—guess what—those clothes!

There turned out to be close to sixty boxes of them, I guess. Actually I lost count. We stacked them about five high in ten stacks, and those were just the tagged clothes. Her hats and shoes and handbags filled up another couple of stacks. The boxes were big, too, the ones that held a few dozen of those three-roll packs of Wal-Mart paper towels each. Other things that she wore or just hung or laid regular in her chests-a-drawers, we laid out carefully on top of the stacks —— well, after we aired them out or ran them through the washer and dryer. Each stack of boxes ended up topped with about six or seven pieces of something or other, but we took pains and made it all look neat.

And covering a couple of the lower boxes, out in plain view, was the jewelry. I wanted the family to see it first thing, with no hint of our holding back anything. But it really was pitiful. I have to say Miss Mattingly had god-awful taste in jewelry. It was all in gaudy colors and as fake as fake could be, so fake it couldn't pretend to be real, but it was all there was, and we set it out fancy, on cotton in boxes or in the original ring boxes and other holders when we could find some. I figured her kinfolks would want it for mementoes anyway.

Gwendolyn Aurora Mattingly had been a hundred and six when she died, somebody told me, and I do believe she looked every year of it even a long time before that. I only saw her way back when my momma and daddy and I came to town on Saturdays like everybody did back then. I was kind of scared of her, to tell the truth, with that wild light gray mane looking as though she had got caught in the wind and it pushed her hair up.

She would be sitting far back in the back end of her big brown car, a hulky Packard sedan that was about a hundred years old itself even back then, I think. Her brother that drove her around sat perched up on his seat, hands gripping the steering wheel and eyes straight ahead. His pinched face with its pointy nose put me in mind for some reason of a chicken. He was so tiny I wondered how his feet touched the pedals.

And in the back seat with her was the biggest, ugliest tan color dog I ever saw then or now. Its slack-jawed head looked like it would hit the inside of the car roof, and the dog was sitting down. It looked around at the people outside on the sidewalk in front of the First National Bank, where I had just been with my momma and daddy. There was a big nowhere look on its face, and its mouth was open and slobbers hung down both sides.

His teensy little owner looked the same way, not with the slobbers, but she looked all empty and nowhere too, and she didn't even look out at the people.

Miss Gwennie, I heard that the nice society ladies called her, took that dirty brown muzzle-faced dog everywhere. I never knew where she was going or being taken, and those were the only times I ever saw her.

You know, I've always heard it said that "clothes make the man," and I guess it could be applied to a woman, too, but what that mess of clothes ever did for Miss Gwen, I still haven't figured out. As I said, she was kind of a mystery.

But now I bet I knew more about her than most people in town ever would, except Mayjo maybe. You can't say you don't know somebody personally if you have been handling their drawers for a solid week.

Drawers? Oh, I reckon you might call them underpants, or panties. Now, I can't believe I'm talking to a reporter, and a man besides, about such as that.

After we were all ready and waiting, the family finally got there. The nephew, who seemed to be the spokesman, was already pretty age-y himself. I reckoned that he was the son of the tiny man, Miss Gwen's brother, who used to drive her around. The nephew was short and kind of fat. He walked with a stick, and his clothes smelled like Ben-Gay. I know that smell from home. My husband Perry has to use it often when he gets home from work. It's not easy hefting and carrying bags of fertilizer and horse feed and such and loading it into customers' trucks all day long.

"What in the world!?" blustered old Amos Mattingly, Miss Gwennie's brother's boy, well, an eighty-year-old boy. "What is all this?"

Some other kinfolks that I didn't really try to get names from were crowded up behind Amos, and they were all staring at the roomful of clothes that Gwen had gathered up over a lifetime.

Mayjo usually takes the lead in talking to clients, as she calls them. I just call them people that we clean for. But she was slow in answering this rude man that I had already decided I didn't like, so I popped up.

"These are Miss Gwen's clothes," I said, just a statement of fact. "And her jewelry is lying out on top." Mayjo still didn't talk, so I just went right on.

"This was all through the place. It's got pocketbooks and hats and underwear and some winter coats and wraps. She had clothes she never put on, still had the tags on 'em," I said clearly, like it was just matter-of-fact.

Mayjo told me later it was a good thing I spoke up. Never would have thought she would say that, kind of bragging on me. But it was true that I did a good thing, it turns out. It came in handy later, what I said that day.

Here I thought that with getting the house cleaned up to this point, our work was all but over. Oh, I hated getting all the clothes out and stacked up, but at least I figured that was the end of them. For some reason I thought all these kinfolks would just up and carry these boxes out of the house. I had my mind set on hanging and beating that braided rug that was under them, just as soon as the boxes got moved off them. But it wasn't that way at all.

"You girls gonna have to do something with these garments of Miss Mattingly's," Amos proceeded to say. I didn't catch it all at first, I was so mad at me and Mayjo being called "girls," like our names didn't matter and like we weren't the full-grown mothers and grandmothers that we are.

"Get them out of here, and quickly," he ordered. He never even looked right at me or Mayjo, just kind of above us, which is where I guess he thought he was. "Take them where you want, give them to some place that takes them, just don't let me see them sitting here in the floor when I get back tomorrow."

Mayjo was struck dumb again. And she was two years ahead of me in school. I reckoned I would have to take on the talking if we did more jobs together.

"What do you mean?" I demanded. "It's not our job to do that. We were just hired to clean out the house. The bank man called up like he always does when there's somebody who dies that hasn't got any...*family*..." I let the word sink in sort of accusing-like because here these buzzards were, only coming in after Miss Gwen's money anyway, if she had any.

Mayjo found her voice, right in the middle of what I was saying. I sort of wished she wouldn't, I was on such a roll and kind of enjoying the funny looks on the Mattingly kin's faces.

"What she means is…uh…" started Mayjo, but then didn't have anything to say after all.

I knew exactly what I was saying, though, and I kept on.

"What I mean is what I said, it's not our job," I continued, gathering up nerve like a rolling pin gathers up piecrust dough.

Then I went and did it. I said too much, but I just couldn't stop. Maybe it was the way Amos's eyes looked like they were going to pop out, or maybe the smirky little laughs that came out of the strained-faced middle-aged women on his right and left. But the good-looking young man in the background was standing, just listening.

"You'll have to pay us more," I said it quiet like but oh, so clearly, "and what's more, you'll have to sign something that says we have the right to take the clothes out and they'll be ours to do with how we want."

I was thinking, I dread touching the heavy things again, but if it'll get the best of this old goat and we get paid for it besides, I can make myself drag them down to the Goodwill myself. It would take about five trips in Perry's pickup truck and him grumbling about it every time, but I would get him a little something nice with a piece of the extra money I would be making at clearing the clothes out of the house. Just not all of it.

Amos Mattingly looked like he would start to fuss, and then caught himself. Oh, I had already figured out that he had to get the things out of the house in order to sell it and divide the money with his sister's two daughters, the snooty women on his sides. So, right then and there, he said what he tried to say later that he didn't.

"You bet I'll sign something," he blurted, almost laughing. He tore a little piece of paper off a plastic covered pad from inside his suit coat and started scribbling on it.

"Here," he shoved the paper at me. I read it, though it was written worse that my first two grandkids could do in second and third grade where they were, and it said, "To whom it may concern, clothing G. Mattingly is prop. of bearer." It was signed "A. Mattingly." And there wasn't a thing about any extra pay, like maybe I was dumb enough to have forgotten that silly, unimportant detail already.

Well, I didn't like that. I spoke right up, too.

"That's not too precise, wouldn't you agree? I'd appreciate it if you wrote it over—and put in about the extra money," I said, biting my words off so he couldn't help understanding.

This time the young man was laughing. Not at me, though—at the red-faced man who was, what, his great uncle, maybe?

And if I thought the grand-nephew was good-looking before, well, he just about turned into Robert Redford when he opened his mouth to talk.

"Uncle Amos, I'll write it up better and get it all witnessed," he offered, "and these ladies have done such an excellent job so far, I know you will want to reward them with a bonus, and also pay them for the removal of the boxes. I'll be glad to work it all up and notify the bank to pay them the extra."

Amos just stood there red and puffy in the face, and the middle-aged women didn't look any too happy, but I would have sure been proud of this handsome, smart young fella if he had been my son or even kin to me any way at all. He sure knew how to talk and how to be considerate of people. But maybe that's not too important to some folks.

Mayjo, when she got where she could talk again after being afraid of the hateful little man, well, she let me have it.

"Laveda, I can't believe you did that," she hollered right after the four family members left that day. "I don't want one thing, not one thing, in that whole pile!"

I was thinking, well, I didn't want it either.

"You're crazy," she kept on yelling, "if you think I'm moving one of those boxes to MY house!"

Well, that made me mad, because I thought for a minute Mayjo was going to try to back out on the rest of the deal I had just made, and the extra money would all fall through.

And because it made me mad, I found myself talking out again.

"That'll be fine, Miss Mayjo," I answered all cold and calm, "but you'll have to sign it away. I have to have things done proper and legal."

Mayjo looked funny, like I had hit her. We didn't say any more about it that day.

The young man was loyal to his word. The next day Mayjo and I were working on some clean-up jobs out in the front yard of the Mattingly house. He drove up and had with him some professional-appearing papers, written with words pared clean so that anyone could understand, and also a lady from the courthouse to witness and put her notary by the signatures. He even had a paper from the great-uncle naming the young man, Jeffrey S. Tibbets, to sign for him.

I explained that Mrs. Merrick—that's Mayjo—was no longer part of the deal except for being paid for her extra work, and he said "No problem" and wrote her right out of the clothes deal and had her sign off on a paper.

So that's how I ended up owning all the clothes, not anybody else.

I sometimes wonder what Mayjo really thinks of that today, even though she always acts glad for me.

"I thank you ladies on behalf of my uncle," Mister Tibbets said with a kind of regretful smile, "even though he didn't do it himself."

As he packed up his copies in a neat little burgundy briefcase, I couldn't keep from smiling at him. Mayjo was still rattled and had pretty well given over to me on doing the talking for us both.

"You did a nice job," I said to him as we shook hands. "Your great uncle and the two ladies—one of them your mother?—(He acted almost ashamed, but nodded "yes")—ought to be proud of you."

So the legal part was done, and couldn't have been better. Betty June Dougherty works in the courthouse at the county attorney's office, and she checked for me. It was done up as tight and pretty as any piece of lawyer work, she told me.

Now to the clothes themselves. The things we had laid

out would have to be packed up, too. You can't really go taking loose clothes in on your arm to a donation place, at least not this many. I can't say I was thrilled at searching out more boxes and stuffing them, but now at least we would be paid for the extra work, and by the hour, too. The bank said all they needed any time was just our word on how many hours we used.

I never cheated on anybody I worked for, and fudging on hours would have been just like stealing, I figured. So we still worked fast and made all the time count, though we could have stretched it out. But it took the rest of the day, anyway, to get it all packed up to be moved.

And then I beat the heck out of that rug.

Now, you're not going to believe this, but I got it all home in a matter of an hour or so at the end of the day. Perry didn't even get a chance to fuss, as I didn't have to borrow his truck anyway. Mr. Tibbets, that kind young man, sent over a box truck and a couple of workers to load it all and take it to my house and unload it again, right into the back bedroom.

I bet Perry wanted to divorce me. He had just cleaned out Debbie Ann's old room to put in a den, like he said he always wanted, and here he came in the house after work at Southern Farm Supply, and in his would-be den were all these boxes stacked up two-thirds of the way to the ceiling.

"Why didn't you jist take them straight on down to the Salvation Army or the drop-off at the Catholics?" he demanded.

"I have to go through 'em," I answered, as sweetly as I could. I wished there were some men's clothes in it, so I could promise him that, but there weren't any. "These consignment places, they have to have it all sorted by season and sizes, I found out, and even the Salvation Army and places need it divided up some so I can get a receipt," I told him.

He pulled his hands through his hair and went on in to the living room to watch the Channel 6 news.

I started on the loose clothes. In two piles, I placed several newer summer tops and some casual clothes for Debbie Ann and Gloria, our older daughters. Most of the really expensive-feeling slips and bras were full-cut, so I divided the best ones between them. Not that the girls are that large, but Miss Gwen was just so small. (I did put the old holey underpants in the trash.)

Another pile with mostly play-pretty things was for Gloria's baby girl, including a little lacy cap and a shawl like they must have worn in the early days to keep warm in the house. Brittany would maybe just sleep on the wrap or drag it through the house now that she was walking, but that was okay. I got it all free anyway, you might say.

Let's see, now, there was another pile for Sherry, my baby even if she is twenty-two. She's slender and sexy, but she still couldn't wear many of Gwen's clothes, being as the older lady was so teeny. I figured the shoes ought to fit her, though, and I picked the ones that had barely been worn, and were of new enough styles. It was an effort to make Sherry feel good. She had been kind of depressed since the guy she was halfway seeing shipped out with his Army Reserve unit for some peacekeeping and they had about quit writing, and I figured she might need a little pick-me-up like cute shoes that are stylish and look expensive. And there were lots of the really silky undies that did fit Sherry after all.

Another pile was for Perry's mother. She is tiny, even more so than Miss Gwen was, and the fluffy bathrobes and housecoats kind of bundle her up, but she looks awfully cute in them. I know she likes them because every time I go over there now, she comes to the door in a different one. She even fixes herself up more, though she stays home all the time.

I started to notice something. This was turning, without my even noticing at first, into something good. Of course there were boxes and armsful of things that we took straight on to the Salvation Army. To be helpful, I made sure they were pressed and sorted.

Another pile was for the teenaged daughter of the woman who just started to our church. I had noticed that she liked the "look" that was around when my two older girls were teens back in the 70's and early 80's, and she was tickled to death with Miss Gwen's double-knit stretch tops and a pair of her clunky-heeled shoes. At the last minute I added a funny floppy hat. I'm really glad I did. That little gal loved it all, and I got a big hug from her. Her mama thanked me, too.

But I had only scratched the surface.

The hats got loaned out to the ladies' mission circle for a fund-raising tea party. Some of the women modeled the crazier ones and had hours of fun. The people who showed up without hats had to pay extra, above their admission, for a hat to wear. I didn't let them be bought, though, except for the ones that had been repaired a lot. I did a pretty good job at fixing them up, I have to say. Nobody but Mayjo and me knew which ones the repaired ones were.

Miss Gwen's everyday coats and wraps had just a small amount of wear to them, and I sent them right along to the Goodwill. Well, not right along—you should know me by now. I made sure the buttons were on tight and anything that could be fixed, was.

Oh, the list goes on and on, what with sweaters for the health care home, some dress-up clothes for a school play, help for a lady that was burned out of her home, and so forth. But the best was yet to come.

I think I told you about my youngest, Sherry, and her breakup with her boy friend? She had just moped around long enough, I guess, and one day she met up with a nice guy and started seeing him. I could tell she was being especially careful this time, but I knew from the outset that Wade was going to be okay. I think it was because he smiled with his eyes, not just his mouth. Didn't hurt that he had a kid's face still, and I bet his hair was red as fire when he was a kid, 'cause it had some color to it even now.

And he sure did turn out fine.

"Miz Stiller?" he started, even though I had said call me Laveda, "Miz Stiller, have you ever thought about getting a computer?"

I laughed in his face. I really did. I hated Miss Bradley's typing class way back when. Why would I want to do that again?

But I tried to be nice. "Well, Wade, I don't believe I have. I'm probably too old."

Now, Wade is bashful, but he kept trying, to his credit.

"I...I could do it on my computer," he kind of mumbled. I didn't know what he was talking about.

He went on. "You see, Laveda," I was glad to hear him say my name, "there's a way to sell things on the computer. And..." he chose his words..."those things that are still with their tags—and even the receipts by themselves—are just the types of things that some people want. They call it 'vintage' clothing."

I know I stared at him, but I was just trying to put this all together with little Miss Gwennie's clothes when he said something else that about floored me.

"And the white, flat boxes, especially those that have the store names on them, just make them worth more. You do know, I reckon, that all those stores weren't around here, just a few of them. The rest were in places like Lexington and Louisville, even some all the way to Saint Louis and Nashville," he explained.

What! And I had come close just a few days earlier to putting all those dusty containers in a great big fire.

I had heard Sherry showing him the piles of cartons and had wondered why a young couple would waste time standing in a room of old clothes and talking for an hour.

Now, I'm sitting here telling you this, and I know you heard about what happened or you wouldn't be here asking me about it and writing it down. But there are details you might like to know, like Paul Harvey always says, "the rest of the story."

I just trusted Wade, and I get people right nearly all the time. He did me fair and got me started on this internet auction. You know the one I mean.

We all got into it. Perry got pretty good with the camera, I made sure the clothes were just so,—you know how particular I am—and Sherry did the descriptions. She was always clever with words and English, but seems like she has just got better and better through doing all this research about clothing types and styles. Wade did the computer end of it all.

"I need to be doing something," I fussed. "Only thing you all are letting me do is hand-press out these things and double-check that they're clean and all fixed. But you know that I can call every little stitch and spot on these clothes, as much as I've looked at them since this summer."

So they put me to holding up the clothes or they would take my picture fixing outfits up on the half-mannequin that Debbie Ann found for us. They insisted on standing me and it out in front of my chicken house. Now, I like showing off my flowers and my chickens and the funny yard signs I painted, but it didn't go with clothes selling. Anything to keep peace in the family, though.

"This makes no sense a-tall," I said. "Who wants to look at me when they're dialing in to see the clothes?"

But folks watching their computers must not have minded me being in the pictures.

The day I thought I would have "The Big One," as Fred Sanford always used to say, is when Wade and Sherry came over to the house on a Friday afternoon. The computer was at Wade's apartment, and I suspected that Sherry and he were on the verge of living together. I didn't like them doing that and not being married, but I had kind of my ESP going and I was seeing signs of them getting it legal.

They came in holding hands, and I thought, "This is it! They're gonna get married."

I smiled over at Perry and tried to wink without the kids seeing me.

Wade said, "Laveda, maybe you want to sit down? Sherry and I have something to tell you."

Just like in the movies, I thought. I acted so innocent,

and said, "Oh, my, whatever can it be?" and smoothed out my skirt and sat on my red plaid sofa. I was ready.

Oh, no, I wasn't.

Wade said, "Laveda, you know the dress, the one with the dropped waist and the short skirt, the one like you said your momma wouldn't have been caught dead in, or her daddy would have killed her if she was?"

"The flapper dress?" I replied slowly, wondering what in the world a flapper dress had to do with these kids getting married.

"Yes, that's it," interrupted Sherry, and she couldn't wait any longer.

"It sold last night on the auction, and it brought four hundred and eighty-three dollars!" she almost shouted.

Well, I was still a little behind, I guess. It was like I heard it but didn't. I think I was still ready for the engagement announcement.

I know I acted the fool once I did get it straightened out in my mind. First, I thought somebody was playing a game, but when the money order came—that's just like money, you know—I figured it was real.

Then the camisole, the one that Mayjo and I had giggled about, being as Miss Gwen was a maiden lady and that piece was a sexy number for sure, well, it went and fetched a hundred and four dollars and thirteen cents. (I don't understand where those odd-penny numbers come from, but Wade says it's something about the bids, where people tack on just a little more to beat out the other people that are trying to buy something.)

And on it went. The 1960's pillbox hat that looked just like Jackie Kennedy? Well, it brought over forty dollars itself. A tie-dyed shirt with "Woodstock" across it, that I had a fit over them even putting on the auction because of the holes in different places, brought seventy-nine dollars and some. I made sure Sherry called every one of those holes when she wrote it up, and Perry fussed, but I made him take little-bitty closeup pictures of some of the worst ones. That way I relaxed partly, but not all the way until the money order and the good feedback came in.

I could tell you more and more. Oh, there were the two ladies in Lexington who set at each other over a handbag that came from an old store that closed there years before. Seems their mothers had told them about it, and that it was where the really rich horse-money women shopped back then. And that name was one that I just assumed was an old store right here in Luten. Good thing Wade had a sister who had lived up in the Bluegrass region and helped him with the store names. I guess Lexington is probably at least about a couple hundred miles away from us, even if both towns are in Kentucky. It's like we're in two different worlds, with Lexington being a big city and all.

Anyway, those two ladies fought it out over that sad-looking little strap pocketbook. It was made out of kind of a metal mesh, to beat it all, to where you could almost see in through the sides, and it was old, old. The metal on the snap top had words that stood up and said some name like White and Davis. I hope that the lady who won the bidding didn't get too sick at herself for spending a hundred and eighty-seven dollars and change on that little swingy thing.

The jewelry—you know that god-awful ugly jewelry I told you about?—ended up being just the stuff that these crazy collectors wanted. I made Sherry tell that it wasn't real, although people starting paying for it just like it was. But the gaudy, loud pieces were the ones that brought in the money. Some bangle type bracelets were just plain old hard plastic as far as I was concerned, but turned out to be something called Bakelite, that made them really special. "Love beads" from the sixties and "mood rings" from the seventies were hits, too. And up until then I had always thought, like I said, that I could figure people.

It took about six months of listing, picturing, and getting the money and sending the stuff off, to work through Miss Gwen's clothes. After all, it brought in, even after the commissions and fees were taken out, over eleven thousand and sixty dollars!

When the last priority mail package got taken to the post office, I felt like crying and laughing all at the same time, but mostly I felt relieved. I was glad to be rid of that stuff, worn out from the push-push of it all, and ready to claim my house back and fix up Perry's den in that bedroom.

Yes, that's one thing I did with the money, but even after the big-screen TV and two leather Comfy-Man recliners for me and Perry, and some other special things I might tell you about later, there was still enough money left over that—you know me by now—I had most of it put away to help a little on the grandkids' education.

It really did bring us all together. Especially Wade and Sherry. Yep, you guessed it. They got married in April this year, her looking so pretty I about cried. Well, I did cry.

Another thing that made me misty-eyed was the stained-glass window panel that was up behind the preacher, back-lighted and with a cross in the middle over a scene of Jesus praying by a rock, I think in the Garden. Now, you can't put this in your writing—I wouldn't want people to think we were proud—but Perry and I bought that whole setup and had it installed. We made everybody who just absolutely had to know about it—besides us, just the preacher and the workmen—not to ever let it out that we gave the money. So they said it was an anonymous donation and kept it quiet. Seeing Sherry up there with that beautiful scene behind her, her and it both glowing, made the day just about perfect for me.

Something just had to happen, though. Right when the church was filling up before the ceremony, I was looking out from the ladies' restroom where the girls in the wedding party and their mamas and sisters were all dressed and waiting, and I saw somebody who was out of place.

There he was again, that Robert Redford man. It was Jeffrey Tibbets, Mr. Amos Mattingly's grand-nephew! I wondered what he could be doing there, and of course my mind flew to the matter of the clothes. Word had gotten out all over the place by now about how we had gotten "rich" on Miss Gwen's things, and even old Amos had been heard from indirectly. Sadie Smith, my uncle's ex-wife but we're still friends, heard him spout on about how people had made money off Miss Gwen, but she said nobody paid him any mind because they all knew that it was Amos himself who was the very picture of making money off Miss Gwen.

But here was young Jeff, and I had to think it was connected to his great-great aunt's clothes that he was present. Could he be aiming to ruin Sherry's day by claiming the money back for the clothes, on his uncle's behalf? Would he really face me down right there in public? That didn't seem like the kind of person Mr. Tibbets was, but he was so smart and efficient, I was afraid how he had worked for me earlier could be turned around now and used against me. My mind was racing, for so much of the money was already spent and more of it was being spent right then on that wedding.

He came right up to me where I was peeping out the ladies' room door. I scooted out and shut it hard behind me, so Sherry couldn't hear anything that would upset her wedding day.

I braced myself and said politely, "Well, hello, Mister Tibbets. I sure didn't expect to see you today, but I'm so glad you came."

See, I don't know how they do things where you're from, but here we just put out word in the paper that all "friends and family" are invited to a wedding. Now, in Luten, Kentucky, that means everybody—whether they know you or not—will find an excuse to go, for the chance to look around at who's there, and for the free food afterward. And even if that's why they come, well, so what? It's a day to be generous and welcome everybody. Therefore, I meant just what I said.

He nodded his head ever so graciously, putting me in mind of a bow, almost. His blond hair that sort of fell over his forehead and that toothy dreamboat smile made him look harmless enough. About that time he said the most amazing thing.

"Mrs. Stiller," he said, "you are a genius, the way you marketed that old clothing. I am so proud to know you. You are an American success story. If you weren't a married lady, why, I would sweep you up to the altar today myself, even while your daughter is getting married."

And then he kissed my hand! I couldn't talk, just blushed, I'll bet, and people around me, even the girls spilling out of the restroom by now, were all clapping and hollering, "Yay, Laveda!" and stuff like that.

He was only being a gentleman, didn't want anything, not any money or any recognition. Now why can't the world have more people like that in it? I never saw Mister Tibbets again after Sherry's wedding day, kind of sad to say but somehow perfectly right, too, because the story of the clothes was over that day, too, as far as I was concerned.

Just one more thing, though.

When Perry and I got back home from the wedding reception, we made popcorn and sat in our Comfy-Mans and watched "60 Minutes." I got to thinking about how the story wasn't really over, after all. Somewhere in a motel room in Paducah, Wade and Sherry were showing little Miss Gwendolyn Mattingly's undies the time of their life.

Printed in the United States
46689LVS00002B/433-531